There is no way to know when they will approach you.

Likely it will be in an aisle you've only just started to explore. It will probably be a woman.

Note how she looks. If she wears black-framed glasses and a pink cardigan, it may be a positive sign, or a lure. If her manner is gruff, and her hair is tied in a bun and her fingernails are long, you are not welcome.

She will be running a finger along the spines. Make a recommendation if you can. Be sure you are holding this guide in plain sight. Speak with passing casualness. Make no accusations, demand no exceptions. Allow her to see your pain.

If she nods politely and turns away, you have failed your application. Do not think that you can try again. It is better to have come this far and failed than to try the Librarian's patience. Accept the mercy and come away.

If the lights go out in the building, run. Drop the guide and go. For whatever reason, you have rung bells in the Library Beneath the Streets, matched a pattern they recognize, and they have decided you are too dangerous to allow. You might get away before the walls switch around and the shelves close in and your spine is locked forever. There are stories of those who have escaped, but not many, and they never stop running.

The LIBRARY

Beneath

The STREETS

TaLes of the surreaL and the wondrous

by

DANIEL HALE

ZUMAYA OTHERWORLDS · AUSTIN TX

2018

THE LIBRARY BENEATH THE STREETS

© 2018 by Daniel Hale

ISBN 978-1-61271-368-7

Cover art © Bob Hobbs

Cover design © April Martinez

"Zumaya Otherworlds" and the griffon colophon are trademarks of Zumaya Publications LLC, Austin TX, http://www.zumayapublications.com

Library of Congress Cataloging-in-Publication Data

Names: Hale, Daniel, 1990- author.
Title: The library beneath the streets / Daniel Hale.
Description: First edition. | Austin TX : Zumaya Otherworlds, [2017] |
    Identifiers: LCCN 2017014290 (print) | LCCN 2017033649 (ebook) | ISBN
    9781612713694 (Electronic/Kindle) | ISBN 9781612713700 (Electronic/EPUB) |
  ISBN 9781612713687 (softcover : acid-free paper)
Subjects: | GSAFD: Fantasy fiction. | Horror fiction.
Classification: LCC PS3608.A545685 (ebook) | LCC PS3608.A545685 A6 2017
  (print) | DDC 813/.6--dc23
LC record available at https://lccn.loc.gov/2017014290

DEDICATED...

To the writers who showed me what a good short story could do: China Mieville, Neil Gaiman and Ray Bradbury.

And to my father, Tim Tucker, who showed me what a good artist should do.

TABLE OF CONTENTS

THE LIBRARY
BENEATH THE STREETS

D'shall had restless fingers. On the right, they drummed in steady rhythm against the smooth surface of the binder he held in his hand. On the left, they shook so badly he was obliged to keep them in the pocket of his coat. Even that carried some risk, he knew—what he intended would be no easier to achieve if they suspected he was armed.

He was prepared to kill. He'd gone that far before, although never for the sake of a story. Tonight there would be no avoiding it.

D'shall was not experienced in the theft of stories. It was a secretive art, a discipline all but unknown to even the most disreputable dens. Not surprising, when successful acquisition held no guarantee of payoff. Stories are an infinite commodity, worth nothing but for the telling, and the will to tell. This is the secret.

And the time a story is told is as important as the story itself. D'shall knew this, which is why he waited while his hair of silkworm strands retreated across his scalp, and his restless fingers ground his aching knuckles, and his shattered, clunky teeth were dyed to jaundice by too much coffee and too many cigarettes. In that waiting, he dug deeply for the lore of the story thieves.

It amounted to little more than a handful of minor names—literary footnotes who had found there was little satisfaction in passing off the work of another as their own. Some, as atonement, had then moved on to try penning tales.

But the doubt of storytellers is a sickly taste in its purest form, and becomes an acidic bile on the tongue when tinged by thief's guilt.

The lengths to which they went were often more fabled than their perpetrators' names. There was Reynolds, whose efforts to cultivate Poe's ravings drove him into a lethal delirium. There were the four Watsons who each claimed to be the doctor Doyle pretended to collaborate with and then tried in their own ways to claim damages for Doyle's injudicious authorship. There was the small roster of names of those who had professed responsibility for kidnapping Agatha Christie, for drugging her into a fugue, or for wooing her so effectively that she feigned amnesia to protect their identity.

D'shall was the best of them. Or, he told himself, he would be. Not for him the half-true boasts of absurd effort, nor even the single shanghaied idea-turned-masterpiece. There was a grander prize, whose custodians he awaited in his cold attic room.

It had taken years just to put him on the right track. The break finally came from Bell, a near-shiftless drunk who nevertheless carried a ratty notebook full of unfinished sonnets and snippets of prose.

It had once been D'shall's strategy to befriend the aspiring ones, in the hopes they might suddenly be inspired to show some effort. He'd gotten nothing for his troubles but tirades of self-pity once ideas fizzled out. He couldn't escape the man, either, after being ready with a round and an ear. That was enough to keep more promising prospects away, and it was less trouble to keep buying the drinks and tune out Bell in silent commiseration.

Bell had been remarkably quiet that night, sprawled in his accustomed slouch on the table. There was a distance in his eyes, emphasizing the wildness of his haggard face and dirty, unkempt beard. It discomfited D'shall, who'd come to rely on Bell's litanies as a soothing background hum, and so he was moved to ask him what was wrong.

He'd written something in, as he put it, a sort of daze.

"I wasn't sleeping good," he told D'shall. "Meningitis, the doctor said. I'd taken some medicine, you know? A couple different things. Thought I'd see what I came up with." He gave D'shall his notebook.

D'shall flipped to the last few pages, peered at Bell's cragged handwriting.

"It looks like a list."

"Dunno what I was thinking. I was going for this tragic artist thing, I guess? Sort of a *Graveyard of Forgotten Books*, but in reverse? I dunno." He sipped his beer more readily, and stared off gloomily into nothing. He did not notice when D'shall pocketed the notebook.

At the start, he could not have told you why the strange piece arrested him so. For all his failed pretensions to the artistic, D'shall was a solidly sensible man. The lore of story thieves was fraught with its own share of unlikely miracles and literary Holy Grails and outright anomalies. There were as many mystics among them as there were plain opportunists. Most often, they were orphaned adherents, robbed of their faiths after decades of callous practicalities. What they looked for in stories was the unnamable, physical chord that rang shockwaves in bereft hearts. They sought the foundations of faith.

Of course, many of them soon became aspiring messiahs and spread their usurped words like narcotics amongst the likewise downtrodden. But a few believed the stories spoke of—or spoke into being—new truths. Then, their dreams became ones of purposeful quests, long voyages in search of the nearest thing to magic as they could get in this world they'd tired of so long ago.

This is what D'shall had been waiting for; he knew that now. He'd been patient for the start of a masterpiece—not a half-finished fable he could take what little credit there was for himself but a seam that would lead to an ocean of fortune. Why else should he find it from the pen of a thing like Bell, an otherwise hopeless louse who was too familiar with his own failed opportunities to recognize what he had?

This was a truth, baldy written as it was.

He'd followed the words carefully, and it had all borne fruit so far. He could still remember the dream of the old woman who glowed like corpse flesh, who'd spoken to him in a voice like the whisper of wind through cobwebs. And now her servants were coming to lead him to paradise.

A twitch in the shadows. D'shall was tired, despite his excitement. But he stood from his bed and faced the corrupted wraiths that were suddenly with him. He held the papers over his chest, like a talisman.

How to Join the Library Beneath the Streets

1. *To begin, you must find this guide.* You have choices.

Feed the pigeons with the ginger-bearded man who walks with an iron cane.

Speak to the tired woman with the yellow helmet who sleeps on the bench outside the diner.

Enter the cinema five minutes after the final show. Sit in the empty theater and see what appears on the screen. Look under your seat.

Follow the trail as far as it can take you. Sooner or later, if you have not tripped an alarm, they will tire, and you will find the guide somewhere you can get it.

Do not despair. Do not abandon the tedium of the quest for sake of a shortcut. There will be no hope for you then.

Do not be dissuaded. Years of work shall be undone by the slightest doubt.

2. *Go to the library as often as you can.* Take the guide with you.

Never stay for longer than an hour. Never check out fewer than four books. Do not linger on the choices, nor dwell on preferences. The knowledge of the Library is often buried deep in the words, often obscure and esoteric, and always widely spread. You must appear to be casting your net wide.

You may find something suggestive in the marginalia. Ignore it—if there are genuine secrets the Librarian was fool enough to let slip, they vanished long ago, smothered by the mildewy stacks. Anything you may think you find is like to be a trick, or a trap, or your own imagination. Ignore it, and remember: this is the safer route.

You will not know if they are watching you. Do not try to uncover the transmitter embedded in your library card. Do not try to free from the book a bound soul who defied the Library, kept in bondage and psychically bound to the Librarian. Do not challenge the sorters to a game of riddles. None of these rumors are true.

The Librarian will soon know of you. Not a muscle will move on her paper-pale face when she does. Her lips will not purse, her brow will not crease. She has known your like before, and you do not surprise her.

You will be in her books now.

3. *There is no way to know when they will approach you.* Likely it will be in an aisle you've only just started to explore. It will probably be a woman.

Note how she looks. If she wears black-framed glasses and a pink cardigan, it may be a positive sign, or a lure. If her manner is gruff, and her hair is tied in a bun and her fingernails are long, you are not welcome.

She will be running a finger along the spines. Make a recommendation if you can. Be sure you are holding this guide in plain sight. Speak with passing casualness. Make no accusations, demand no exceptions. Allow her to see your pain.

If she nods politely and turns away, you have failed your application. Do not think that you can try again. It is better to have come this far and failed than to try the Librarian's patience. Accept the mercy and come away.

If the lights go out in the building, run. Drop the guide and go. For whatever reason, you have rung bells in the Library Beneath the Streets, matched a pattern they recognize, and they have decided you are too dangerous to allow. You might get away before the walls switch around and the shelves close in and your spine is locked forever. There are stories of those who have escaped, but not many, and they never stop running.

If she smiles and asks you to tell her more, rejoice. You have bought yourself a little time. It will be no easier from here.

She will tell you she is a member of a small book club that meets in a disused boardroom in the library every third Saturday, and invite you to the next meeting. Accept—the interview is concluded, and you have qualified for the follow-up.

In the Library Beneath the Streets, the Librarian stands at a lectern and gives an order. The thunder of typing fingers is like a rain of bones against the rooftop of the underworld.

4. *The book club is a scripted dance, a pretension to normality.* They may tempt you with opportunities to share your knowledge. Do not be tempted; the streets are not inviolate. The Library Beneath the Streets is the sanc-

tuary of the world, and it must be kept sacro-sanct.

Watch the discussion—the old lady who writes fan fiction based on Wild West serials will insist on sharing her current project; the sallow-faced young man in the black clothes who sits by the window will verbally abuse any book that was written after the nineteenth century; the red-haired man who moves his hands as he speaks will use words like *dichotomies* and *juxtaposition* with every sentence.

Your associate from the shelves directs it all, encouraging discourse and inviting comments, an able-bodied maestro; but remember this is already carefully orchestrated.

Know your opening. Do not speak over the others, even when it seems that, at any moment, discussion will erupt into violence (pay attention to the black-clothed young man if you think you are doing poorly). Your friend will invite you to say a piece when it seems you are not saying enough. Do not try to impress, do not talk like the red-haired man, or show insincere admiration for the old woman's stories. Do not try to get the black-clothed man to expand on his views. You are here to be heard, not to listen.

Your patience will be of use. The change will come subtly. You may know it, but do not let it show on your face. Ignore the sounds. Do not stumble from the sudden lurching of earth. Do not hesitate at the sight of darkness blanketing the window.

Every point raised and question asked will be posed to you. Answer quickly, do not hesitate, do not wonder at the right answer, do not try to embellish your knowledge, if, indeed, you are even capable of it at this point.

Ignore the noises of clanking gears and falling earth.

Ignore the shaking table, and the photos falling off the walls.

The members of the book club will seem to straighten and thin in flesh. Their eyes will be still. Their lips will compress to concrete lines. The Librarian has noticed you.

If you have done everything properly—and if everything you have done to get this far has been sincere—your head will begin to hurt. Your hands will shake, your nose will drip with blood. Your brain will feel as if it is boiling on the outside while a lump of ice seethes on the inside. A fever of revelation will be lapping at the edge of your consciousness, and the pain will be all the greater when it leaves you just short of total understanding.

The end will not come at once, but will fade away like a dream as you rise from this uppermost corner of the Library Beneath the Streets. You will find yourself awakening in a cluttered office room, returned to the daylight streaming through the windows. You will not know if you have passed, but take the fact that you have been returned to mean that she needs time to think about you.

You will not know. Wait to be contacted.

5. ***Do not blink when the Librarian comes to see you.*** She will seep from the shadows like a phantom made of dust. Do not bother to hide your dread.

She will begin to question you, without preamble. She does not stand on niceties; everything she asks will be frank and straightforward, and you will not recall a word of it afterward. This is for the best—she is asking everything that shows you as you are, and you will find yourself unable to lie. Your eyes will stay on hers of their own volition. You will remember nothing but the pull of her eyes, and the distant sound of her voice.

Her voice is a terrifying thing. It is not the inhuman shriek you would half-expect from such a wraith-like figure, but quiet and even. There is this about it, however—it cannot be swayed. Whatever the Librarian asks for, she receives. She has made demands of empires, ensnared the culture of entire civilizations. She persuaded the original inhabitants of the Library's subterranean passages to leave, and kidnapped and coerced dozens of lost tribes into expanding the chambers, digging deeper and deeper into the earth.

They say she told Mount Vesuvius to hold off on erupting until she could walk off with a few choice volumes, and convinced Alexander to burn his own library (she had the originals, and would not allow copies to exist). She killed Gutenberg for his blasphemy, and will not hear mention of Garamond.

When she asks you her questions, you will not speak falsely or fail to give information. She will know how you found out about the Library, and what has urged you to seek it out. She will ask you of your home life, the patterns you have seen in the books, your wants and your regrets. She will ask you where you were when the person closest to you was suffering, how many breaths you take before you go to sleep, the farthest you've been from the moon, and why cats walk on the other side of the street when they see you.

You will answer all of it truthfully, without understanding your own answers. If you have not been entirely sincere, it is too late to regret. If she sees anything in you she finds wanting, you will have no way of knowing immediately. She will not merely reject your application; she will see you as a branch to be pruned. You will be stripped, snipped, chipped, mulched and pulped into fertilizer to grow the bindings in the Library Gardens.

In a way, it will be a victory. You will have joined the Library, and it will likely be the less painful path.

If, however, she finds you acceptable, she will only purse her lips and nod (they say the skin will tear from her skull if she ever smiles).

Then you will blink, and she will be gone.

You will remember nothing but the suggestion of the smell of book mold, and the fluttering of pages.

6. *Give them your life, without regret.* Do not discover a new will to live. It is too late.

7. *The first time she sought volunteers, the Librarian played songs to call them.* She took children from places that forsook knowledge on principle, because nothing so changes the world as a muse borne from ignorance. This had the effect of spreading a seed of forewarning in every place she stole from, forcing others to look beyond their prejudiced minds to try and understand. Tragedy breeds caution, caution breeds logic, logic breeds imagination. This is how the Library cultivated us.

You will need no such enticement. She will send her servants to escort you.

Sleep as much as you can. They will come in the night. Consider how comfortable you would be to see where you are going.

Keep the lights off. They do not like to reveal too much of themselves. They are so pale they glow, blood-starved lichens, but they do not like to remember.

They will seem to bleed from the shadows, congealed pearls of putrescent flesh. These are your predecessors. They gave all they had to give and were remade for a new task.

Do not stare too long at them, and do not keep them waiting. Leave your bed unmade, do not take anything with you.

Tell no one. They will not think of you when you are gone.

The streets will not seem the same. There will be no lights on.

You will see the Librarian's servants easily, moving at a somnambulist pace, unhurried but determined. Do not touch them if you can help it—they are mostly bent to the Librarian's will, but they are savage beings. They do not react well to surprises.

You will come to a staircase as the street seemingly ends. Follow the servants downwards, and savor your last taste of the world above.

She will be waiting for you at the bottom. The servants will hurry away, relieved to no longer be under the open sky they abandoned so long ago. Do not speak to her, ask no questions. She knows everything she needs to know about you, and you know by now what is to happen. She will turn to the tunnel behind her. A few bare bulbs light the way, but there will be no time to adjust your eyesight.

8. *You are here now.* Be proud. It is nearly over.

Do not rush in. It is dimmer here than in the tunnel. The tellers do not need to see what they are doing. The words are in their heads.

Relish this victory and take in the sight. It is everything you hoped for, exactly as you imagined. Every writer is the image of the purest concentration and devotion to the art. Imagine yourself in their fever-bright eyes. Imagine every fault of body and mind you have longed to excise from your person.

Relax now. It will all be over soon.

Listen to the typing, constant and unceasing. This is the sound to which the world is re-made again and again. This is the place where the dreams that shape civilization are put to paper. These are the people who have sacrificed everything to be the ones to write the narrative to which reality is scripted. Now, for all your unceasing concentration, you will join them.

You are nearly there. There is one last thing you must remember—do not struggle.

Let them strip you of your clothing; there is nobody here who wants to see.

Let them strap you to your chair before your typewriter. It is normal now to be afraid, but do not show it. Prove to them that you have forsworn it all, and that you are ready.

Once they place the first paper in your typewriter, she will whisper in your ear. You will know what she has to tell you, and hear it in your bones. These are the words you have wanted to live by all your life. Now you will.

Begin. Do not hesitate as the letters bite into your fingers; type through the first sting. Let

them sip your blood. You are beyond the con-
straints of physicality by now. You will pen
your words by your blood alone. You will pour
your soul into the stories of this and every age.

Remember this victory.

Remember as you lose yourself in the world
you are told to build.

And when the bad nights come, when your
lesser-self wakes up screaming in a nightmare
of its own devising, when the Librarian comes
to quiet you, when it happens, remember that
you are where you wanted to be.

To his credit, it gave him pause. It was easier than it should
have been.

The dream of it was headier than he'd anticipated; to watch
the guides seep forward in stop-motion movements from shadow
to shadow was to watch an absurdity. D'shall's attempts at writing were a distant and unpleasant memory, but he remembered
the protracted battles between mind and word, trying to limit on
paper the mad spectacles that plagued his sleep. It was his failure
in this that disillusioned him of his own capabilities.

How to do justice to the bled, papery creatures that came for
him in the night? How to describe their robes like monks' sack-
ing, elongated tails suckling at the ground like the frills of mol-
lusks?

And then: the street he'd walked a thousand times, undulating down the spine of a city he'd never known to be so quiet, lapping concrete-turned-sea-turned-stairs into a deeper darkness, before the promise of a flickering light?

D'shall panicked. He could not complain, really—the instructions were ephemeral, vague. But he'd expected the old woman
to be waiting at the foot of the ramping streets, ready to lead him
through the shadows and to a biting typewriter. He'd expected a
palpable threat, not the murmured promises of the night.

He had a blade, a slivered piece of silver folded from an heirloom plate. It was a molten dagger now, stinger-sharp and wicked.

No longer would he discount the trope of knowledge hidden in fiction. Inherited silver. Simple sharp edges. One or the other would do the job in a pinch.

But there was only the darkness, and D'shall had lost sight of the escorts in his distraction. Had they dissolved to an even hazier substance? Were they even now flanking him for ambush? Had they sussed his intentions?

Dark held no horrors for D'shall. He took off in bullet intent, melted silver clasped in hand (somewhere he'd dropped the papers). He kept his eyes ahead, tried not to stray from the forward path to the light.

It was not a great distance, but perspective seemed reluctant to settle. The light wandered in zigzag configurations with every step he took.

He wasn't sure how close the walls were; his steps echoed sharply on the path in ringing marble taps that still seemed to slouch from under his feet, going no farther than his immediate sphere.

The air was not stale, nor musty with the smell of aging paper, nor even mealy with dried-blood ink. D'shall might as well have gone for a stroll of a spring evening, in a park very lightly perfumed by sleeping orchids. It was clear, clean, and almost sweet.

The light did not creep gradually towards D'shall. Indeed, it seemed to him that he'd lost some time in the shadows as he blinked his way into a cavern lit by a warm, soothing glow. It reminded him immediately of some recovered cave in the *Thousand and One Arabian Nights*, untidy with piles of treasure.

The treasure here was paper—great sprawling heaps of paper, tied together and set in stacks. Perhaps a current or a careless hand had brought them tumbling down, and now a great many of them tiled the white stone of the cavern floor.

No sound but the faintest soughing of the wayward winds over bound, dried paper. No fingertip piercing by typeface syringes. No inking birth from blood-womb sorrows. No moaning from failed, sorry artists who thought their pain made them special. Just stacks and stacks of ripe material.

No more pause. D'shall came with no real plan in mind, no idea what he'd get hold of. His own literary tastes had long since withered into irrelevance, more concerned as he was with what others liked. He knew it was largely a matter of luck, in timing as well as location, that determined what proved readable.

Still, a badly written story tended to transcend subject matter objectively enough to spot. Best start reading.

He chose a pamphlet at random. It was tied with a brown, rubbery cord that looked disgustingly organic to his eyes. He drew his molten-silver knife across it, snapping it as easily as an elastic band. Then, sitting cross-legged and getting comfortable, D'shall read...

THE SNOWFLAKE
COLLECTOR

When the snow started, Matthew didn't wait. He was out there the first night as it fell, trying to keep his hands as still as possible while he held the piece of black construction paper. He was shivering a little—this work was too cumbersome to do with gloves, so he kept one hand in his pocket, next to the magnifying glass. When he had enough, he brought the glass out, and carefully and quickly scanned the flakes that had fallen on the paper before they melted.

Lots of Ds, it looked like. Maybe one or two As. It was hard to be sure. He had to catch them quickly and wipe them off before the paper was soaked. He had plenty to spare—there was a whole ream of it in the house. But it was best to make it last as long as possible before he had to run inside to replace it. He didn't want Suzie to think he was leaving.

It was her favorite winter game. When other kids were having snowball fights or building snowmen, she was standing very still with her sheet of black construction paper and magnifying glass, catching snowflakes to look for messages.

"How could there be a whole message in a snowflake, princess?" he would say. And she would frown and speak slowly in that grim, no-nonsense manner of hers. "It's not a whole message, Daddy. It's just one letter."

So, he bought her a little notebook to keep track of the letters. Once they filled a page they would take it inside to see how many words they could spell from them.

He hated winter more than any other time of year, but he loved his Suzie. He would endure anything, even frostbite and run-ny noses, to keep from disappointing her.

Never again, he swore to himself.

The sheet was sodden and soggy now. He caught sight of the final letter just as it was dissolving.

Y! His knees almost gave way with relief. She was calling him, she really was!

"Daddy's here, sweetheart," he whispered. "Daddy's read-ing them just like he said he would."

He flicked the wet paper off his fingers, then stuck them un-der his arms. The door opened behind him; Justine stood in the doorway, wearing her pink bathrobe, clutching the ends tightly around her to stave off the cold.

"Matt? What are you doing?"

He resisted the urge to hesitate, as if caught doing something indecent.

"I'm...we're talking, that's all."

Her face hardened before the words had even left his mouth. She sighed.

"Matthew, please don't do this."

"Yeah. Suzie and me." He tried to stay casual, keep from get-ting angry. He knew Justine wouldn't understand, had hoped to do this without her finding out. She was a worrier, over-protec-tive and fearful, always at a loss of what to do with Suzie's outgo-ing, inquisitive nature. "You wanna get me a new sheet? She prob-ably wants to say hi to you, too. I haven't seen any Ms yet, but—"

"Matthew, for the love of god!" She stayed in the doorway; her face had gone red, and little tears were peeking out from the corners of her eyes. "Don't do this!"

He turned his back to her, and spoke to the air.

"Suzie, honey, how about you make Mommy a heart, like you did on Valentine's Day? I bet she'd like that."

———

Justine's reaction didn't surprise him. She was the polar opposite of their daughter, utterly reserved and uncertain. Suzie skipped and ran; Justine shuffled and skulked. Justine spoke with an even, reasonable voice whenever Suzie was acting up, but Suzie spoke right over her, for all intents and purposes oblivious to her mother's scolding. Matthew was the only one she would listen to, if only because he would do everything she said.

Justine was a good mother. It was just a shame that her daughter was too energetic for her.

"*You* watch her," was all she would say when Matthew tried to get her to join in on Suzie's games. "You watch her, and make sure she's all right."

———

The skies were clear of snowfall the next few days. Matthew didn't care; he sat by the window, staring at the sky, waiting for the smallest flake.

Justine was in the other room, talking to somebody on the phone. She did that a lot nowadays, although Matthew hardly took any notice.

"Won't even talk about it," he heard her say, and "Soon. Please."

It felt like minutes had passed when a new voice spoke.

"Matthew?"

A man's voice. He turned away from a promisingly dark mass of clouds to see a thin, bearded man in glasses standing in his living room.

"Matthew, I'm Dr. Guyer. I work with your wife. She called me to come and talk to you."

Talk? He didn't want to talk to this man. Not when Suzie was on her way. What was Justine thinking?

"Talk about what?"

"Well, whatever may be troubling you, for example. You've become somewhat distant, and we—that is, your wife thinks it might do you some good to talk about things."

To hell with it. "Did you see any snow on the way here, Dr. Guyer?"

"Snow?"

"Yeah."

The man paused, apparently baffled by Matthew's asking after the weather. Clearly, he had come in with some kind of script prepared and was already finding it hard to follow.

"Matthew, perhaps we can talk about your daughter."

Matthew turned back to the window. "I haven't spoken to her today."

"I...ah. Well." Dr. Guyer coughed discreetly, mentally back-pedaling to regain his professional footing. "What do you and, ah, Suzie talk about?"

"That's none of your business. Justine!"

"Matthew, I really do think a talk would do you good—"

"I'll wait till Suzie gets here, thanks. You might wanna talk to Justine, though. She's been kinda weird lately."

The clouds were close now. Matthew took up his paper and magnifying glass, ignoring Justine as she came into the room.

"Matthew, what...?"

He pushed past her and stepped back into the cold.

◆

Justine didn't bring it up again. From that day on she barely spoke to him. She was still speaking with Dr. Guyer; Matthew would see her in the window, talking on the phone with her back turned to him. A small part of him suspected what was going on, and what would likely come; but the rest of him was too devoted to his correspondence with Suzie to care.

She occupied his every thought now. He tried desperately to recall the happy, cheery dynamo his daughter was before she grew sick. It angered him beyond words that the clearest mental image he had of her now was of her lying in the hospital bed, ghostly pale in the thin sheets, clutching weakly to his hand while he sang to her, "Here comes Suzie Snowflake, dressed in a snow-white gown, tap-tap-tapping on your windowpane to tell you she's in town." She would smile, and the obvious toll it took on her brought a hitch to his voice.

They had been past the point of hope for recovery, although Matthew ached for it. He pleaded with the doctors for some shred of light, had broken down in tears in front of Suzie when the truth finally sank in. Justine would not come—she'd begged that it was too painful for her to see Suzie reduced so. Matthew could never forgive her for that. Suzie did not ask where she was.

"I'll write to you, Daddy," she whispered. "When I get up there. I'll ask someone to teach me how."

He kept his hand on her forehead; she was cold, and shivering slightly. He stroked her damp hair and promised he would find her messages. He would read every one, just like the ones they'd found when she was well.

"I'll make them simple," she said. "'Cause I know you have trouble reading them."

He had to laugh at that. When they played the game, he would always pretend to see what she saw—the minute pictures carved into ice crystals, words and faces and microscopic cities. She hadn't been fooled.

⊷

The blizzard hit the second month. At this point Matthew was spending every spare moment he could outside, collecting the snowflakes. His face was getting chapped, and sensitive. He wore a scarf over his mouth, sunglasses, and a hood over his head. By now his hands were frozen. They no longer shivered as he held out the paper.

Work never called to ask what he was doing, and he saw no reason to tell them.

He pursued the messages as a prospector would approach a gold seam, with infinite patience and indifference to his surroundings. There was no doubt in his mind he was communicating with his daughter, even if he had yet to complete a whole message. He'd found a G, and an A, and an R, and another D. Maybe Suzie had met her grandparents? That would be a nice thought; Matthew's mother had died just before Suzie was born, and not being able to see her first grandchild had been her only regret.

He ignored Justine when she walked stiffly down the front stoop (he hadn't shoveled), dressed in her long coat and carrying a suitcase.

"Matt." She was speaking up, as though he were deaf. "Do you have your key?"

He kept his magnifying glass over the paper, looking for a P.

"Get out of here, Justine."

"You shouldn't be out here much longer. Promise me you'll go inside soon, okay?"

Justine showing concern! It almost made him laugh. Where was that concern when their baby girl was wasting away in a hospital bed, and she was cowering at home?

"You know my mother's number. You know where to find me. When you've sorted yourself out, I hope we can try to..." She paused, her formal, neutral tones at last failing her. "Matt, for fuck's sake, look at me!"

She reached for him. Matthew twisted, tried to shove her away, and the paper flew from his hands. He tried to recover it, but it jackknifed into a puddle of half-melted slush. It was soaked through in seconds.

"God damn it! Stop interrupting her!"

"She's not there, Matthew!"

"Shut up!" He didn't want this, not another word from her, this failure of a parent. She'd let their daughter go and expected them to go on with their lives. She'd wanted rid of Suzie, Matthew was sure of that now. "Just shut up and let us talk." He picked at the mush the paper had become, then turned to get a new sheet from the house. "Go to your doctor, Justine. He seems to have all the answers."

She scooted past him, up the stairs and in front of the door. Matthew shrugged and turned back.

"Matt, he suggested a trial separation to help us deal with our grief."

Our grief? When did she ever grieve? Suzie wasn't under the ground for a day before Justine was back to carrying on as normal, musing about dinner plans and new curtains and yoga.

"You're leaving her for him."

"You know that isn't true! Can't you see how hard this is for me?"

He shook his head, scooped up some snow in his hands and held them out to catch the messages.

"I showed them to you. You wouldn't read them."

"That's because they aren't there!"

"Hey." He squinted into his cupped hands. "There's some more Ms in here. She's asking for you again."

He balled the icy mush in his hands and threw. It hit Justine square in the face. She fell to her knees, crying and trying to wipe the mess from her face. When she pushed herself back up Matthew was already back to catching his letters. When he turned around she was gone.

———

Matthew had stopped using the papers; now he could read the letters in the snow beneath his feet, scores and scores of them he had missed. They were still too jumbled to be coherent, the wind tossing them every which way. But he could see what they were meant to say—lot's of Ds were piled around As and Ys, and there were Ms. He wished he could write back, tell her that Mommy had just gone to see Granny.

He spent most of the next day panning through the snow-drift, which is why he didn't notice at first that no new letters had appeared. He spent the whole night standing in the blizzard, reaching for every flake as it tumbled down to him, and all through the next morning. The clouds were thick with ice now, dumping whole bucketfuls of snow. He retrieved his magnifying glass, removed his sunglasses, panned every inch of the ground. He removed his coat, looked over every flake caught on it. Nothing.

"Come on, Sue. Where'd you get to? What's taking so long?" A blurry film kept passing over his vision. He wiped his eyes, shook his head, but it still persisted. There weren't even any Ds left.

The snowdrift was waist-high now. Matthew knelt next to it, digging and digging for some scrap of message, some indication that his Suzie was still writing to him. Had she given up? What if she didn't know he was even looking?

"No, baby, no. Come back. Hold on just a little longer."

His hands kept on digging while his body slumped to the side. For the first time in weeks, he realized how numb he was, in his face and all through his joints. He couldn't feel the snowflakes settling on his cheeks, or the tears that froze out of his eyes. He couldn't even close them.

"Daddy's here, Suzie. I promise I'll read them all." He could see nothing but the white now, glaring and calm. "Mommy will, too," he promised it. "She just had to go away for a bit."

Matt didn't know when he let go—it was that easy. He just let the wind hold him, carrying him into the white, letting him tumble and picking him up again. He slid through the air, a seven-pointed speck of ice. The cold was everywhere, but he was part of it, and it protected him.

At last the white began to dissolve, wisps of clouds metamorphosing into the nothing. When it gave way beneath him, he could see the whole of the neighborhood. The houses, ugly lumpen things, were capped with snow, made pure and fine. Plows chugged along the streets, churning away the ice to recover the roads. What a thing would it be, he wondered, to be torn up by one of those?

But he did not fall there. The wind was carrying him down, past windows frosted in swirling ferns, past yards crisscrossed with shoveled paths. It carried him low to the ground, dangerously close to the drift.

When he saw her kneeling in the snow, bent over a misshapen wretch half-covered in snow, the wind urged him on with new strength. She wore a thin, pale paper gown, almost invisible on her corpse-white flesh. He was pushed into her hair, stiff and stuck with crystals. The last thing he knew, before melting over her ear, was her voice.

"Daddy? Are you cold?"

The insipid sentimentality was not entirely to D'shall's liking, although the madness fueled by grief and despair had promise.

He set it aside, and reached again for the pile nearest to him. This next pamphlet was slimmer, and shorter.

MENAGERIE
OF THE
PERSECUTED

The exhibit is a scrawl on the map,
A faded image of a building stashed
Away in a far corner of the zoo.
Down a path from the heron's pond,
Squatting like a bunker against the wire fence.
Over the path, the sign reads "The Persecuted."

More shack than sanctuary, all weathered
Boards that look truly weathered, not careful
Fakes of fiberglass turned jungle huts. Cracks
Are stuffed with rags of cloth and hay. Broken
Windows look to be draped in heavy blackness.
The battered door is closed.

Opening, I see shadows jumping in firelight.
Candles set in sconces on the walls lead off
Down the corridor. But I've only a moment
To see when I hear the shrieking, flapping
Flock stirring overhead. The heavy door slams
Behind me, and the shrieking dies away.

No guide to lead me down the path, not even
Maps left as afterthought. No signs to warn
Against camera and commotion, children un-
    attended.
Nothing at all like the zoo's ordered wildlife,
All nature's beauty declawed and tame.
Just the candlelight, and the hall.

The light turns my eyes to dreamers,
Makes them see insect shapes scurrying
Along the wall, across the floor. The dreams
Creep in; affected drowse twists my legs
Around half-seen columns of ants and beetles,
Winding round my drunken steps.

One hand on the wall, tentatively tracing
The way, till I arrive at the first cell.
I see only deep-sea blackness behind
The glass, not a glimmer of shape at first.
When it clears, I cannot tell if it's my
Eyes' widening, or subtle light's reveal.

The cell floor is covered with blankets,
Torn and befouled, littered every which
Way on the cold concrete. Tufts of
Black fur in greasy, matted piles, speckled
With drying blood. I imagine buzzing
Gnats hopping and feasting in bliss.

Six black cats lie in muddled heaps,
Breathing shallowly and licking dried
Wounds of pus and gore. Not a one of
Them with a full coat of fur, only two
With eyes unclouded or intact, not more
Than four whole ears among them.

The sight lasts long enough to put me
In mind of stepladders and shattered
Mirrors, of cracks in the walk and salt
Over shoulders. The light fades, or my

Vision clouds, only the faintest glimmer
Of an amber eye. I move on.

The candlelight does not reach the
Heights of the hallway. I've no
Idea the size of it, but I can feel a
Vast cavern hidden in the rafters, alive
With hanging, leathery shapes. Noses
And ears twitch as I pass below.

Light in the next is a fiery orange, but
The glass is cool to the touch. The same
Pale concrete, steeped in the spirit of
Confinement. But the floor is full of
Writhing life, coiling and slithering
And hissing life, wrapped in rainbow scales.

Frills unfurl at my intrusion,
Fangs bare, tongues make to taste
My sweat on the air. But I can
See the peeling scales spotted rust;
I can see the torn tails and the
Broken teeth and stumbling sways.

Some of the snakes have legs—
Stumpy, half-formed, brittle things
Crooked and broken. They look
Jammed in the serpents' flanks,
Stuck in their sides like sticks
Impaled by children in spiteful glee.

It wasn't by choice that Temptation
Entered the garden. An offer accepted
Led to a life of hugging warmth from
The ground, in a body built without
It. Wickedness incarnate was tacked
On later, by necessity. Such is politics.

It comes to me, as I move down dim
Halls beneath wing-haunted roofs,
That every human evil given face

Has horns or hoofs or snout or fur
Takes flight on night skies or slithers
In the dust, remote or removed.

I find waterlogged rats shivering
In a dampened pit. Itching intensity
Bites into my skin, sends it shivering
At the sight of drooping, dripping
Whiskers. A crier tolls his bell,
Cart wheels splash on puddled cobbles.

Cracked beaks caw frightful in
My ear, crush mouse skulls and
Nuts on a busy street. Clouds of
Shot raises the flock to fury.
I duck beneath a grinning figure
Standing staked and crucified.

Darkness in the final cell fades faster,
Revealing a pauper's terrarium
Of sickly sheened trees and ferns.
Torchlight rushes searching in the brush.
Drums beat, blades clang, feet stamp chant;
The jungle-in-miniature all the more absurd.

I see the animal clinging to a branch,
But I can't name it. Its fur looks as tattered
And torn as the felines in passing, its eyes evil
With yellow. It clings to the branch with
Tiny, immaculate hands. It raises one clawed,
Skeletal digit, and points it straight at me.

Torchlight erupts in the faux-jungle.
Voices tightened with anger scream
To me. The skinned and pinned
Flap like flags overhead, deadfall
Bones crunch beneath my feet.
The air tastes rank and wild.

Nothing will change when I
Leave the Menagerie of the

Persecuted. I'll still think nothing
Of a thousand feral deaths borne
From fear in beastly face. It's all
Beyond my need to care.

Only now I see the terror that
Makes us start at shine in night.
Now I wonder at the scratching
Behind the walls in my home.
Everything I suspect about shadow
And chance might as well wear fur.

THE MIASMATIST

There were no emergency services to speak of in Goria. Its
people had lived too hard to believe in the charity of others,
and were inclined to deal with their emergencies personally.

There was no police force; Gorians are an "easy come, easy
go" lot, and not overly inclined to acts of unpleasantness, if they
do not serve some artistic or ulterior purpose. Murders went un-
investigated, and justice was sought-for quietly. Domestic distur-
bances (such as they were; Gorians give love too freely to commit
for long) fizzled away into the background hum of the city. Fires
were a problem, but the river Faith Breaker was generally but a
short walk away, and in this place of paper sketches and fuming
chemical collages, bucket chains formed quickly.

There was medicine, after a fashion. Like everyone else in Goria, its practitioners were confined to fringe arts and holistic treat-
ments. Diagnoses were considered a matter of personal taste. From
herbalists to phrenologists to enthusiastic home-electricians, it
was considered the right of all citizens to choose the treatment.

Robent Valimo was the only practicing miasmatist in the city.
He had no number in the phonebook, and no fixed address; he lived
on park benches and in open doorways. The better, he always said,
to know the air.

Today he was ambling along the Alley of Birds, hands in the pockets of his dirty smock, and wondering what to do for lunch, when he pulled up short. He sniffed several quick, worried sniffs and renewed his pace, nose poised.

At the end of the alley was a short, squat building painted a vibrant yellow and looking rather like a large block of cheese. There was a closed garage door set in one side.

Valimo banged his fist on it.

"Nivade!" he shouted. "Nivade, open up! House call!"

The door lifted, revealing first the legs, then paunch, then broad shoulders, and finally the bullish, block-shaped head of Michael Nivade, proprietor of the Din Den.

"What's this about a house call?" he asked. "Nobody sent for you."

"Indeed, sir, somebody did. As I said, it was your house!"

"What?"

"Can you not smell it? Come to that, can you not taste it? Your home is crying out, Michael, a-shrieking foul night air. Something has tainted your home, sir, and I am here," Valimo finished with a flourish. "I am here to put things to right! And I shan't charge you more than a hot meal and drink to be going off with," he added.

Nivade looked levelly at the scrawny miasmatist.

"Out," he said flatly. He began to slide the door back down.

Valimo ducked beneath it.

"Oh, dear, the reek of it! You really do not feel it?" He waved a hand in front of his nose, his face scrunched in evident disgust. "Your dear establishment is positively fugged with bad air! Why? What has happened? Has some calamity befallen you, dear Michael? Are you a fiend who has buried his victims beneath his bar and befouled the atmosphere with dreadful miasmas? Speak, man, speak!"

"Get out before I put you out!"

"Now, now, my friend, I'm sure there'll be no need for that. Indeed, I cannot say that anyone here would object. Because, as you well know, the only ones here are you and I! You have no customers."

It was true. On a Friday evening, the Din Den should have been thumping indiscriminately to tunes loud and raucous, solemn and bawdy. There should have been musicians on the stage, and customers shouting to be heard around the tiny bar, all of them in miserably high spirits. Instead, the lights were low, the bar was bare. There was nobody on the stage.

"Well? Am I wrong?" Valimo prodded Nivade in his generous stomach. "Your custom is keeping away in droves, because you have fallen to plague. Tell me I am wrong."

The barman's scowl deepened, and at last he sighed through his bulbous nose. "I've had almost nobody in a week. I had bands booked. Had to let them go. Can't afford them now." He allowed his worry to show. "I dunno what happened."

"Then it is lucky for you," said the miasmatist, "that I was passing. Pour me a drink, good tavernkeeper, and tell me how it began."

Resigned and slumped, Nivade moved behind the bar.

"A few regulars dropped out of sight," he said, pulling a mug beneath the tap. "I didn't think much—"

"Oof! Hold it, Michael, hold it!" Valimo leaned over the bar, hand now covering his mouth and nose. "What is *that*?"

"What, this? It's beer, doctor."

Valimo pinched his nose as he looked into the mug. The liquid was brown, and foamy, and smelled like hops; but that, Valimo knew, was just the surface smell. Beneath that, the stuff smelled of foulness and rot.

"Where did it come from?"

"Local brewer. Cliquor, he called it. What's the problem? It's been selling good. Or it was, at least. I thought it might pull back the regulars."

Valimo shook the mug, watched the cliquor swirl.

"Cliquor, you say? As in C-liquor?"

"Yeah, that's right. Some guy was here a few nights back. Gave me a case, free of charge, and a number to call if I wanted more."

"Did you...taste it?"

"I'm teetotal, doc. But I gave out a few free samples, and they loved it. Ran out well before closing time."

"Hmm. And would this be just before your current lack of business?"

"I suppose so. Just about, um, six or seven nights back." Nivade blinked his piggy eyes. "Hang on. You think it's the beer?"

"I think that might very well be a pertinent factor, yes," Valimo said carefully. *C-liquor.* "Would you happen to have this man's number?"

"I do, yeah, but it's been deactivated. I'd been wondering how to get hold of him. If this guy got my customers sick…"

"I think it best that you leave this matter to me, Michael. And perhaps you could furnish me the addresses of a few of your regular customers?"

"Why? What good can you do?"

"Dearest Mister Nivade! I am this city's sole expert on miasmata. And this mata…" He proffered the mug. "…is miasing very much, I can tell you. For the good of your business, and your customers, you must tell me, that I might stop this sickness from spreading!"

Begrudgingly, eager to get this madman out of his bar, Michael wrote down three addresses for the miasmatist. Valimo assured him he would personally see to it that this matter was settled, that reparations would likely be made to him for the damage done to his reputation, and thanked him for a packet of crisps he had pocketed, before hurrying away.

⊰⊱

The rot hung on the air, heavy and tender. Clay could feel it coating his skin in a fine layer, and under his fingernails. He tasted it on his tongue, meaty, and sweet.

Supply was not a problem. The graveyard was unsupervised, those interred within buried by family and friends. So long as he stayed out of sight as much as possible, he would be left alone.

It would be time soon to collect a new supply. He picked up his bucket and spigot.

⊰⊱

Valimo called upon Reather Haines at Grinder's Hall, Salacia d'Quirel at the Ornester, and Mave Mauve in the basement storeroom under Stabby Bridge. He did not need to stay long to confirm his suspicions.

Haines was perturbed, but like Nivade could not stop the miasmatist from bustling in.

"I must say you don't look well, old fellow. Coming down with a bug, are you?" Valimo flared a nostril. "Rather a large bug, I would imagine."

36

"Just a fever." Haines' voice was shaky; he was visibly trembling. "Or a stomach virus. I've been puking a lot."

"You've had a hard night, by the sound of it. At the Din Den?"

"I haven't been there in days, man. Only had one drink."

"Ah." Valimo questioned him further, then wrapped him in a blanket and left him to his bed, with a pitcher of water and glass in easy reach. He would be dead in days.

D'Quirel was a trickier case. Valimo knew her to be a larger-than-life sort of person in every sense of the word, and her apartment confirmed this—her houseguests lay on every horizontal surface, sprawled, groaning and snoring loudly, while she sat in their midst looking fresh as a daisy.

"Oh, I don't go to the Din Den much, hon," she told him. "Noisy place. Not intimate enough for my tastes. But yeah, I did stop by about a week ago when I was out with Lizal. I'm not much of a beer drinker, but they had this new blend I found simply de-*lightful*. Tasted like absolute sick, but it made me so *tiddly*!"

It was difficult to say. The disease might lie dormant for years, or, which Valimo considered more likely, Salacia's much-abused body would eat it away to nothing. He kissed her hand gallantly and stepped over her guests to make his departure.

Mauve did not answer his door. There were no lights within. He could not be sure with the river so near, but Valimo thought he could detect the beginning traceries of *the smell*.

All in all, he had little enough to do.

There were many who would call Valimo a crook and a con-man. Even in a city of outcasts, his antics wore thin. His theatrical pretensions, his patter, his doggedness—all of these contributed to it, but that was the point.

Miasmatism was not a demanding discipline; all that was really needed was a fine sense of smell. Valimo's was very nearly preternatural, and there was one smell he knew better than any other.

❧

The cemetery was overgrown with ivy and weeds; greenery choked the wrought iron fence. Statues of every kind—gargoyles, cherubim, and others more garish and less identifiable—stood watch over mausoleums and pathways. It was a romantic's idea of a graveyard, wild, melancholy and massive.

Normally, the smell would be masked by the soil. Now there was the faintest whiff, slight but nonetheless there, lingering like an estranged lover on the wind. Valimo doubted that anyone else would notice it, or would think much of it if they did.

Putrefied flesh, human and, he guessed, fairly ripe. Night air.

Valimo smiled, and strolled through the cemetery gates, whistling happily, seemingly content to wander amongst the dead.

<hr />

A thick, stringy liquid ran from the spigot and seeped slowly into the bucket. This was a new harvest, the donor having been buried only a week before. Clay wondered how the taste would be from an older donor.

Somebody whistled from the end of the tunnel.

"Cooee! Sorry to wake you, but I'm afraid there may be an infestation!" A man walked into the torchlight—thin, mangy, and dressed in a stained white smock. "Grave robbers are such a problem this time of year."

To Valimo, the man holding the bucket looked like a primitive island tribesman press-ganged into a sweatshirt and jeans. His skin was dusky, and streaked with mud. His hair wound into a greasy knot of dreadlocks. He wore a thin beard.

"Have I seen you somewhere before? Your face is very familiar." Valimo stroked his chin, his face a picture of studied intent. "I *have* seen it somewhere. Or, perhaps, everywhere?"

"What?" Clay's voice was breathy and indistinct. "What you want, man?"

"Oh, no, friend. Not me. This has been about what you want." The miasmatist stepped forward. Clay set down the bucket, looking ready to bolt. "Cliquour, eh? C-liquor. Coffin liquor. Corpse liquor! Quite a whimsical turn of mind you have there, eh?"

"Man, I dunno what you're talking about. What you want?"

Valimo eyed the spigot stuck in the roof of the tunnel; he could see the bottom of the coffin peeking through the dirt. "Let me see. You are familiar with the term 'coffin liquor,' yes? The liquefied remains of human cadavers, caused by the disintegration of the cellular walls. Quite a lot of it hangs around in these old lead coffins." He yanked the spigot out of the ceiling; ugly black fluid dripped from the puncture.

"I won't ask you how you came across the phenomenon. You probably don't remember, yourself…I know how it is. Inspiration vomits up the most amazing bits of esoterica, does it not? The knowledge probably rattled about your head for who knows how long, and suddenly you found it breeding some rather unorthodox ideas."

"Man, just…you don't…leave me alone, man." Clay's smile was nervous and sickly; his hands were shaking, waving vaguely in Valimo's direction. "I can't help you, I mean…"

"You can't be doing it for the money. I mean, there wouldn't be a consistent profit margin, would there, if your consumer base dies of raving brain diseases? Even in a city without health laws, it would be a hard sell.

"So. A fancy, was it? An idle fancy that you whiled away wondering at. Beer made from corpses. It didn't take cunning to come up with that. Nobody watches the cemetery, after all. It would just be a matter of mixing it up in your own still and passing it off to our dear Mister Mike Nivade, who runs a clean bar despite his lack of imagination."

"You don't know…"

"Ah? Then it wasn't just a fancy, it was a statement! Oh, I *see*. I *understand*. What was it, then? This statement? What does it symbolize?" Valimo stared expectantly at the dithering wastrel. "Come, come! I am agog! Do share your vision with me!"

Clay blinked, his mouth hanging open, and did an odd sort of shuffle from the foot he was leaning on to the other, as if he had tried to get a running start on smartening himself up and had overshot.

"It's…it's all death, you know?"

"What is? Do tell me, *man*."

"All of it, man. It's all death." He smiled, warming to the subject. "We are. It's…the city is, and the world, too. We're walking dead, and we build dead cities. Build 'em on dead people, too!" He clapped as though congratulating himself on an unexpected bit of brilliance. "We eat dead things, and we drink 'em! Mix 'em up with our blood and piss and shit and spit and just drink it all. And then we piss and shit it back. And do it again!"

"Ah, yes. I think I see where you're going with this. Recycling, that's the way! Because, if we do it with everything else, we might as well do it with *real* death, eh? Have you ever read Oscar Wilde, by any chance?"

"Vampires are the aspiration," Clay mumbled. "Maggots are the cycle."

"Oh, dear. I think you're losing your thread somewhat, old chap. Well, never mind." Valimo wielded his walking stick; it was thick, and slightly heavy. "Best get on with it."

He whapped the stick across Clay's face, sending him sprawling. The youth cried out and collapsed into a crumpled heap, whimpering.

"It's not that I take any personal enjoyment in this, you understand," Valimo said. "This is just my area of expertise. We all of us have our parts to play."

Clay sobbed quietly, mumbling indistinct imprecations. Valimo sighed, and brought the cane down on the boy.

"You are not an artist," he said between swings. "No philosopher. You are just. An unpleasant. Freakish. Little shit." Something cracked. Clay screamed. "Yes, we. Eat dead things. But at least. We. Cook. Them. *First!*"

A fury of smacks. The body twitched spasmodically and made disgusting burbling sounds. Valimo wiped the blood off his cane.

"And you shouldn't eat people," he added simply. "The effects of red meat on your constitution are not so shocking."

The miasmatist gazed dispassionately at the boy's remains. *Death is where we start*, he thought. *And where we go*.

He decided the tunnel would be an excellent place to pass the night—warm enough, and out of the wind. In the morning he would see about filling it in.

The body would not be a problem. He was in a graveyard, after all.

THE FERNS
OF
BELLFLOWER ROAD

There are things you do for family.

They were going away for a few weeks to an island I'd never heard of called Edisto. A paradise of sun, sand, and secondhand bookshops. It sounded lovely; I would have gone with them, if it weren't for my obligations.

I was happy to help them. We hadn't always been as close as we were now, and I was keen to be useful. My summer months were wide open, there not being many conventional jobs I was suited for outside of school. I preferred to take it easy, keep to the quiet with my books and my writing. A house all to myself was definitely appealing.

It hadn't been long lived in. Bellflower Road was a grand bricked street of grand brick homes. Inside were white walls and bare wooden floors. There were books in every room, in stacks or on shelves, more than I could hope to read in my life. Even so, I picked a few interesting titles to tackle in the cozy nook where I'd sit most nights.

There weren't many things I had to do. The cat needed regular feeding; to me, he moved like a shadow freed from his master's ankle, inconspicuously lounging on the bookshelves before bursting into excited chase of some perceived quarry. Although he was a glossy black, save for a single splotch of white on his breast, I usually knew where he was from the clatter of his claws on the floorboards. He rarely let me be, going so far as to lie with me on the futon in the basement, where I slept.

Watering the plants was slightly more difficult. My sister gave me detailed instructions on when to water what, but I'd always had something of a blind spot when it came to greenery. As a consequence, I watched each plant nervously, checked the soil for dryness, doused the leaves as well as I could without drowning them.

The only ones I didn't have to deal with were two big, leafy specimens that stood by the front path. They looked like ferns from some primeval era, a deeper green than any I'd come across outside of the movies, veined with streaks so dark as to be nearly black. My sister gave me no indication about what to do with these, so I left them as they were. They looked healthy enough.

I was happy to be useful.

On the first night, the futon fell apart. It seemed that the house did not want me.

On the second day, I received a visitor—a bronzed, bald man with an impressively droopy silver mustache. He looked like a retired athlete, his muscles giving way to a slight paunch. A rat-sized terrier sat at his slippered feet and stared up at me with a look that was marginally more aware than his master's.

"How ya doing? Maurice Ogletree. I live next door."

Maurice Ogletree. It wasn't the most absurd name I'd ever heard, by far. But it possessed a topsy-turvy, sing-song quality that was fit for a nursery rhyme. It certainly colored my perception of its possessor; I could see him in a circus big top, wearing a spangled leotard and lifting up cartoonish black dumbbells to the thrills of the crowd.

"Just wanted to check in on you. Your sister told me you'd be stopping here for a while. You need anything, don't be afraid to get me."

I don't know why I found the idea so upsetting. It seemed antiquated, a fossil. Neighbors no longer spoke to each other, never mind asked after their wellbeing. I couldn't name my neighbors (a family of four with two small children on one side, a middle-aged woman who spoke to her mailbox on the other).

I tried not to let my discomfort show, smiled at Mister Ogletree, and assured him I was doing all right.

He barely paid attention to me; his head was turned slightly to his right shoulder, as though he were watching something—or someone—that was getting too close. There was nothing behind him but the path.

"She showed you where everything is? Told you how to take care of things, and everything?"

I told him that she had, and once again thanked him for his concern. He nodded once more in a distracted manner and picked up the dog. He left quickly, fast-walking down the steps and over the path, slowing down only after he passed the big, leafy plants.

The third night, I heard something scrabbling downstairs (I had chosen to sleep in one of the other beds). The cat was curled beside me, sleeping soundly. I closed the door, turned away with my head under the pillow.

The fourth day, I called my sister regarding Maurice Ogletree. She wasn't surprised to hear he'd actually spoken to me.

"He's sweet, really. Kinda lonely. Asks after us every day about the house. Always offering to help. Mom's a little weirded out by him, but he's harmless."

I wondered what it was that worried him. I would see him next door, sitting in his open garage with his dog alternately yapping at me and hiding beneath his master's chair. Mister Ogletree looked expectant.

On that fourth day, as I was watering the plants, I found something new. It stood in the small garden, just as the others did. It had broad, flat leaves striped with dark veins. It had no blooms that I could see, and no berries, unlike all the other plants.

I found another that afternoon, this one sitting by the door —same leaves, same veins. It had sprouted from a crack in the brickwork. It was definitely not there before.

I turned to look at the big, leafy plants by the front path. Humidity was rising; I could see a slight fog around them, and in the setting sun they looked menacing, unearthly.

That scratching came back that evening, this time while I was in the living room. I could see the cat sitting atop the fireplace. He was looking over me, towards the front door. It was plated with thick, frosted glass.

I saw a shadow moving outside. It was tall, and lean, hunched like a bird. It strutted back and forth along the porch, making a scraping noise against the bricks as it moved.

The dark cat was arched now, hissing absurdly at the thing on the other side of the door for all the world like it would spare him a second glance. Behind the shape, I could make out something that looked like the two big, leafy plants. Now they were bigger, leafier, all but blocking the path from the porch, and rustling strangely.

The air conditioner died with a clunky wheeze that sent the shadowy shape running swiftly.

I woke the next morning still in the living room. The house was stifling; the windows were thick with condensation. Somewhere close I could hear something buzzing.

Outside was...still the same neighborhood, obviously, but changed. For one, it was so thick with greenery I could no longer see the front lawn, or the brick road. The porch itself was covered in decaying brown creepers. A few scattered envelopes lay there, speckled with rust-colored blotches.

The heat was immense, unbelievable. My glasses fogged. Steam felt like it was pouring into my lungs with every breath.

Far away I heard a high screeching noise, followed by the thumping steps of something massive doing its best to get away quickly.

Inside, I double-checked to see that all the doors were locked. Not that anything out there would be slowed by a locked door, but it made me feel a bit better.

I checked the light switches. No power. Same in the fridge, which was now ripe with the scent of rotting fruit.

The shadow cat twined around my legs, miaowing plaintively. I filled his bowl, and scratched his head to soothe him.

I'd found myself some grapes that weren't too badly gone when I heard a voice calling from outside.

"Anyone eaten in there?"

Ogletree.

"Something took my dog," he said. "At least, I think so. His leash is all torn. No blood or anything. Probably just picked him up and ran off with him. Yappy little rat. My wife left him to me."

I sat in the kitchen, unable to call out to him to let him know I was here, and was listening, and risk attracting whatever was stalking around out there.

"Those plants by the porch," he said. "The two big leafy ones. They must've forgot to tell you to water them. That's what keeps them sleeping, see? They're too wild awake.

"Been here since before your time. As long as I can remember. Weren't the first time this happened. I try to keep my eye on 'em, maybe hint to whoever owns the place to keep 'em watered. I mean, you don't think about plants like those ones, do you? Not unless they're hanging in pots. You don't worry about taking care of them.

"I always hope someone'll take it into their heads to cut them down. Dunno if anyone ever tried. Probably wouldn't work anyway. Roots run deep."

Maurice Ogletree stopped speaking for a moment. Even the cat's ears were perked.

"They don't get watered, they start to remember," he said. "Dunno when they are. Or maybe they're nostalgic. They're powerful dreamers, I'll say that much.

"If you're not dead in there, stay inside, okay? Won't be long before somebody comes down this way and notices. They'll need the industrial grade defoliants again, but you should be okay. I took more than my share of dosage. Didn't do me any harm."

I heard his feet crunching on the gravel drive. From upstairs came the sound of shattering glass. I picked up the cat and ran us both to the basement.

I didn't sleep the fifth night. I heard something snuffling above us. It walked almost soundlessly, but I heard cupboards banging open and things falling to the floor. Shattering, crunching.

It never tried the basement door, but I think it got close.

Day six. My family said they would be gone for ten days, although they might've gotten back sooner. They expected regular updates, and it might worry them not to hear from me. I prayed they wouldn't get back before someone—whoever—dealt with this.

The broken futon sat in the corner. I tried not to look at it; I needed no reminders of how badly I'd screwed this up.

The cat seemed calm enough. There was extra food for him, and at least running water so I would not dehydrate. I tried to tell myself I wasn't as hungry as I felt.

My stomach flexed reproachfully. It would have none of it.

I paced the room, feeling the walls, tapping here, putting my ear to it there. I didn't know what I was looking for—a loose brick, maybe. Somewhere I could pull the walls apart. I could dig with my bare hands if I had to, maybe try to traverse this jungle. But who knew how far it went?

The movement went on upstairs. Was something making its nest up there? I imagined cushions being torn, covering the floor in stuffing, and worse. More than ever I felt the need to get out of there. I didn't want to face them when they got home.

I watched the cat devour yet another can of wet food. He must have been a nervous eater. I regarded the gravy left over on the lid.

I couldn't wait this out.

Thunder rumbled high above me. Would it rain? Ogletree said the plants needed to be watered to sleep. But would this be a normal storm, or some prehistoric downpour they recalled? Would it even make a difference?

I got another drink from the sink in the laundry room, mouth held to the tap. There was a narrow window set in the wall above it, looking out to the garden.

I took one last drink, and thought—the side door of the house was across from the basement landing. The garden was in the back yard. If I could be quick…

I left the cat in the laundry room with an open bag of dry food. One of us should at least have a chance.

There was only the occasional scratching upstairs. It could have been anywhere in the house.

Nothing for it. I made a break for it.

Skittering as something roused itself. It was outside the kitchen.

Turned the latch. The door stuck—chain. I pulled it out.

It reached me just as I was shutting the door.

A claw—black, four-fingered, with barbed talons—stuck in the doorway. A dragon's face huffed wildly at the glass, amber eyes wildly appraising me over a gnashing mouth of gray teeth.

I pressed against the door.

The thing's claw gradually stopped twitching. I eased back a little, and the moment it withdrew I shut the door and ran for the garden.

Titanic palm trees lined the driveway. The heat haze made a fever in my mind; mad buzzing assailed my ear, grits of dirt clung to my sweat-dried skin.

Glass shattered behind me.

The garden was buried. Creepers clung to the garage. A layer of brush obscured the cement patio.

A moment's frantic search found the hose still attached to the faucet. I turned it on; padded feet thudded behind me, the creature coming, snorting and slick.

The spray caught in the snout for a moment…and then fell right through it. Solidity began to wash away, the creature staring at the hose's stream quizzically.

It faded like a mirage, or some property of light on the water.

I uncoiled the hose as best I could. There was just enough give to get to the front yard. I kept close to the house, to keep the hose from snagging.

The big, leafy ferns were massive now. Even in a lawn gone wild with recollection, they stood out like markers—beyond this house, our time is now.

The hose's spray cascaded off a curved leaf. The world tilted, only for a moment. The prehistoric vision flickered like neon before reasserting.

A wail all through the jungle. A beat in the soil. Rustling.

"You ain't dead!" Maurice Ogletree—redder of face, splotched by innumerable scratches but still as hardy as ever—pushed his way through the trees. I waved the hose back and forth, trying to douse the ferns as much as I could.

"All this time, I never thought—" Precisely what he never thought was something I missed in the cry that came from the heart of the wilderness. It was closer now.

Ogletree dived back in. "I'll head them off."

I tried wetting the ground beneath the ferns. Another shift in the landscape, slower this time, as if the scene were being rotated on its side.

A frenzied stampede. The cries of forgotten throats.

A scream as high and primeval as anything the ferns could dream.

A shadow stretched before me. I threw down the hose and turned to run.

Maurice Ogletree's dog bounced on its feet, yipping determinedly.

The big, leafy ferns were chest-high again. The lawn was cut short. Bellflower Road was whole and clear.

The dog kept barking. I resisted the urge to turn the hose on it and let it lie.

⊷⊶

A week after the tenth day, my sister called to ask if I knew where Mister Ogletree had gone.

"He hasn't been in his house. We haven't heard the dog barking, either. We're thinking about calling the police."

I told her I had no idea. The little dog was quiet for a change; I'd bought him a rawhide bone, which he was chewing thoroughly.

"I don't think he had any family. Isn't that sad? Nobody to help him."

And nobody, I thought, for him to help.

D'shall had not noticed as he set each new story on the pile that they wove themselves together, like a novel manuscript undergoing a phantom transition into a book. They were bound by the suggestion of a cover, a hazy aura with tacky substance and a dark, tarry appearance.

The sight was enough to assure D'shall he was on the surest path to wealth. He would have a whole series before the night was over. It moved him to take up the tattered, mercurial book and move deeper into the derelict library.

It really was the most magnificent sight, the Library Beneath the Streets. The thrown-away stories slumped over every surface merely exemplified the grandiosity. There were mountains of the elastic-bound pamphlets. Why had they been abandoned? By what criteria were they deemed unfit to be read? Or had the writers fled, having ripped their shredded fingers from their typewriters and overthrown the old woman, leaving their half-finished works behind in favor of some unknown liberty deeper in the tunnels?

Well, they'd soon regret that, he decided. They were more bloodless than he had thought not to consider taking along a chance of reward for their painful labors.

Humming blissfully, D'shall made his way deeper into the stacks, taking this pamphlet or that, skimming it quickly, and adding it to the growing manuscript under his arm.

LEFTOVERS

"Mitch. Mitch! Pay attention when I'm talking to you, dipshit!"

Mitchell Graves looked up from the fryer, his round face somber and attentive.

"Huh?"

"Take the grease and dump it, dumbass. I don't wanna be stuck here any later than I have to be because of you, understand?" Dave the manager, on grill duty, thrust a tray slopping over with watery grease at Mitchell, splashing his apron.

"Okay." Mitchell took the tray and lumbered out of the kitchen. Dave scowled at his back.

"Fucking 'tard," he muttered, not quite under his breath.

Mitchell took no notice. He never seemed to hear anything anybody said to him when he was focused on the job. He would just stand there, frying fries or washing dishes, working slowly and carefully like he was disarming a bomb. It was a diner, for fuck's sake; it wasn't like it took a genius to do the job.

Dave supposed that being the manager's nephew got Mitch special treatment for being so slow. He had been working there for more years than Dave knew, and he would probably still be there long after Dave had left. He never made small talk, he never complained, and if you did manage to get his attention he would just stare at you with that stupid look on his face. He gave Dave the creeps, that was for sure.

Dave sneered at Mitch's back. He wondered if the moron knew how much Dave hated him.

<hr>

In the back room, Mitch dumped the contents of the tray into a plastic bucket. The level rose to the top, so he heaved the bucket up and exited out the back door to the barrels where the grease was stored for pickup.

He glanced at the security cameras on the wall above the barrels. He knew his aunt did not check the footage as well as she'd used to, and chances were she wouldn't notice if he took the whole bucket. But no, best to play it safe. He removed the lid from one of the barrels and dumped almost the entire contents into it. Then he replaced the lid and went back inside.

The bucket was now a quarter-full as Mitch took it down to the cellar. There, hidden beneath a shelf packed with buns and bread, he had discovered a pipe protruding upwards from between the wall and the floor. A large cork had been wedged in it some time ago. Mitch removed the cork and, with a great air of solemnity, dumped the remaining grease down the pipe.

Mitch knew precisely what Dave thought of him, but he hardly cared. He had more important matters to concern him. He had been chosen for a greater calling, and to stoop to Dave's level would be to betray that sacred duty. He was the instrument of a power Dave would not understand, that Dave's impurities would not let him understand.

No matter. It was no concern of Mitch's.

"Seeping be praised," Mitch whispered down the pipe. Gurgling echoed far below.

<hr>

When you see them, you don't need to be told. You can recognize it in the vacant look, the wide eyes, and the mouth that is open just slightly. If you talk to them, you recognize the halting, hesitant tone and the too-loud voice. It is an easy thing to spot when someone is a little bit different in the head. It is an easier thing to spot those trying not to show that they know.

When you see them, you look away, telling yourself you don't want to stare. In truth, you don't want to witness this travesty, this perversion of the human condition. Only when someone else turns and sees and points them out, only *then* can you regain sight—to defend them. You reprise the role of Good Samaritan, casting scorn on the insensitivity of some people. They must get enough of that, you think. Poor things.

Mitch did get enough of it. He had enough of being treated like a thing, day in and day out. He could deal with the ones who insulted him, made fun of the way he looked and the way he sounded, laughed at the way he wrung his hands in frustration and shook in bewilderment when people got impatient with him. At least it meant they were treating him like a person, albeit one they could bully. It was the others, who looked away the minute they saw him, who spoke to him in condescending, sugary-sweet tones as if he were child—those were the ones he couldn't stomach.

It's very hard to live anything like a normal life when people decide you are not complete.

So, Mitch had resigned himself to his status as a non-person. The best he could hope for was to be the tragic prop for people to practice their compassion on. If you could ignore the artificiality of it all, it wasn't so bad. There were benefits—he kept his job at his aunt's diner, so he could at least feel like he wasn't a burden, even with the certain amount of leeway he was granted. He could never be everything it took to be normal, never be a whole person, but at least he could be useful.

If people got angry at Mitch for how slow he worked, it didn't stop them from turning over the tedious jobs to him—sweeping up, filling the condiments, wiping down the shelves, emptying the garbage cans. Mitch would stay behind and finish the jobs that were not his responsibility, and nobody would question it. So long as it got done—and if Mitch was doing it then it would be done, eventually—then nobody thought to care.

And so it would go, with people being either spiteful or pitying to Mitch, giving him work to keep him busy; and he would pursue every task put to him, alone in his mind and in his life, just as he had been one night in the restaurant, after closing when everyone else had gone home, when his god revealed itself to him.

During the day, the kitchen floor was covered with red rubber mats, in theory to keep the workers from slipping. In practice, the things were such raggedy tripping-hazards it would have been safer to do without them., Mitch took them in the back at closing time and hosed them off. Underneath, the floor was yellowish tile, scuffed and filthy. Mitch dragged a sopping wet mop over the floor, and the water sluiced into the drain set in the tiles.

That night the water pooled over the grate but did not drain away. Mitch looked down at it anxiously. Obviously, the pipe was blocked. He moaned, thinking about the trouble he would surely get in, and wondered what he should do.

Beneath his feet, Mitch heard a low gurgling noise, and a few bubbles floated to the top of the standing water. Swirly strands of a viscous black substance seeped through the grate. Then, the level of the water started to rise, flowing over the walls of the drain and onto the floor. The black gunk was pulled along with it, dragging more stringy strands up from the pipe before meeting a dip in the floor and staying in place. It was thick—it didn't pull apart as more of the gunk was dragged up but coagulated into an amorphous lump. A length of it—an actual *weave* of spiked greasy strands—trailed back down the pipe.

Mitch stared down at it. His mouth was hanging open, and he wrung his hands. He wondered what he should do about this. He wondered which would get him in the most trouble—dealing with the mess immediately without the go-ahead from someone else, or failing to do so. In his experience it was either one or the other. It made quick thinking somewhat difficult.

The lump continued to squat there like a crusty, oozing scab, studded with bits of yellow and brown. More bubbles broke on its surface.

Mitch started and peered closer at the lump. Its body seemed to be coiled into ropey tentacles. Unless he imagined it, the lump had moved...

Thunk. The thing jerked, splashing muck onto Mitch's shoes. He backed away as the thing prickled and convulsed at his feet. He made to bolt, but his fascination—disgusted and appalled fascination but fascination nonetheless—held him still.

The "creature" was covered in short black spines that wavered sickly on its flesh. Its bristly limbs waved lazily in the air, like a recumbent octopus. Mitch realized they were the burnt scraps left over from meals cooked on the grill.

Mitch sat and watched the thing. Fear was easing away, replaced by something akin to awe. Slowly, he raised a hand and reached out.

Snap! A slimy tentacle gripped Mitch's finger. Mitch gaped as a rough, ropey limb slithered over and around his hand, leaving oily trails over his skin. Its slithering movements seemed curious, enthusiastic—almost affectionate.

On some level, Mitch was aware it was very late, and he should be getting home if he wanted to make an early start of it in the morning. But here and now, there was only the creature, and a small yet rapidly growing sense of duty.

This is mine, he thought. *And I will protect it.*

For the rest of the night Mitch stayed at the diner, letting the creature or whatever it was run its feelers over his hands, his arms, his face. He watched as it dragged itself across the kitchen floor, exploring every corner and crevice. By the time he wondered about getting home it was an hour before opening, and he began to panic.

The creature, thankfully, seemed to know this as well, and pulled itself down the drain. With haste, Mitch mopped up the kitchen and replaced the cleaned mats, with only minutes to spare before his aunt arrived. Fortunately, he had a set of keys, and it was not unheard-of for him to get there before her.

She smiled widely at seeing him, and Mitch was surprised that it annoyed him more than usual. It seemed an automatic reaction and empty of meaning. His curt nod in response must have reflected this—Aunt Catherine hesitated, and peered at his shirt. He realized it was covered in the grease and sweat from yesterday.

"Laundry day?" she asked, and laughed uncertainly.

He muttered some excuse, and she nodded before he finished. *Nobody listens. What's it matter what I say?* He headed to the back room for an apron.

Dave was already there, tying one on. As usual, he ignored Mitch—or at least pretended to. *Why do you try so hard to show me that you hate me?* Mitch shook his head and rubbed his temples at the unfamiliar harsh thought.

"Move it." Dave shoved past Mitch, and glared back at him. "Fuck, you stink, man! When was the last time you had a shower?"

"Don't shout," Mitch said under his breath.

Dave turned back, his face clouded. "What did you say? Huh?" He marched up to Mitch and pushed him.

"I said don't shout!" Mitch stood over Dave, uncertain but assertive.

Dave blinked, confused. Mitch was *taller* than him. He usually seemed so small, crouched and shaking like a hunchbacked freak. He recovered himself enough to say "Don't start shit with me," and left.

Mitch's heart was pounding. His fists were clenched. His head, usually clouded over with the urge to be quietly helpful, blazed with something else. He didn't recognize it at first, because he had never really felt it before; but he knew it was confidence.

He heard a liquid sound, like something disturbing the flow of water in the pipes beneath the floor.

◆

Very little changed over the next few months, at least visibly. Mitch continued to pursue his jobs with diligence, only now he was driven by the pride of his secret. Every day he could feel it beneath him, swimming through whatever pipes it needed to be nearest to him. Knowing it was there, watching and waiting, filled Mitch with a sense of assurance he had never known before. It was the confidence of one who knew he was the concern of a Greater Force. It was faith, pure and unsullied.

And at night, when everyone else had left, Mitch would wait for it to rise. When it did he would sit on his stool and just watch it slither and explore the corners of the kitchen. He would marvel at its shape, and the ease with which it crawled about, the spiky chunks of burnt remnants flowing over its skin like so many feelers. It would pull itself as far as it could, an umbilical trail of bile and scraps leading back to the drain. Apparently, it could go no farther than the kitchen. It would occasionally sit in front of Mitch, pulsating and writhing, and Mitch would reverently brush his hands over its skin.

Every moment of every day Mitch would think about it—he took to calling it The Seeping. He thought of the little drips of grease scattered about the kitchen he had never been able to clean —under the shelves, in the corners of the ceiling. He wondered how long it had been beneath the diner, crawling through the pipes. He wondered what could have brought it to life. Most of all, he wondered how long it had been watching before it chose him.

His coworkers noticed there was something different about Mitch, but weren't able to decide exactly what it was. To his aunt it was that he seemed to have a lot on his mind, and was anxious to get back to it, whatever it was. She was rather relieved about that; Mitch had always seemed so devoted to his job that he neglected having an actual life.

To Dave, it was as if Mitch was starting to get uppity. Not in an out-in-the-open sense, but subtly. Whenever he had told him to do something before, the retard would usually grovel like a faggot. He still did what Dave asked, but like it was *his* decision to do so. And he smiled all the time now, like he knew something about Dave he was just itching to hold over his head.

If only he could tell them. Beyond the growing contempt he felt for his aunt and the amused pity he was beginning to feel for Dave, Mitch had few emotional ties to the world around him. His only concern now was The Seeping. Every night he would sneak more scraps and fat for it, helping it to grow. He would see the fruits of his labor as The Seeping pulled itself along by a few more precious inches. Soon it was able to drag itself out of the kitchen and into the dining room.

More and more, Mitch would plunge his hands into the thing, letting it investigate every crevice in his palms and every hair along his arms. An idea was starting to take shape in his mind. He knew The Seeping was intelligent in its way but still limited. There was something of the farm animal in it, sitting placidly in its spot before moving on a little ways and then settling down again. He thought of the years of grease and scraps that had accumulated in The Seeping that gave it its form—the remnants of burgers and hotdogs and chicken, flakes of metal and hair, all sloshing together in a watery mix. The animals that had been made into the food comprising it had presumably not been particularly clever.

Mitch was beginning to feel very firmly what he must do to help The Seeping. The god had chosen him, had made its decision that he was the only one it could rely on for help. He was *chosen*, and he needed to prove himself worthy of that choice. He would give The Seeping what it needed to be greater. To be smarter.

Mitch had to do it. He knew he could. He had *faith*.

It was night. The customers were gone. The waitresses were gone. Mitch's Aunt Catherine was gone. Dave was on his way out.

Mitch kept his head down, studiously scrubbing the counter, as Dave brushed past him to the back door. Technically, as manager, he was supposed to stay behind after closing to make sure everything was wrapped up. That he left without doing so was something Mitch had used to tell Catherine, and that she would always promise to look into. If she did, it had done no good. It was still pretty much a given that Dave would leave early.

Tonight, Mitch was counting on it. He reached under the counter as he heard the door slam back open.

"*Shit!*" Dave rushed past the kitchen and to the office. Mitch hurried after him quietly, the knife in his right hand and the grease bucket in his left, suddenly anxious.

"What's wrong, Dave?"

"You stay the hell away from me right now if you know what's good for you, Mitch. My fucking tires are slashed, and I can't find my auto club card." He was sitting on the desk with a phonebook open on his lap, swiping at the pages.

Quickly, before he could think about it, before Dave could react, Mitch made his move. By the time he was aware of it, he had already stabbed Dave a dozen times in the chest.

Dave gasped in pain and disbelief, and Mitch regained his senses enough to grab him by the hair and hold his neck over the bucket. Gingerly, he slit Dave's throat. A small amount of blood oozed into the bucket, mixing with the bit of water and grease that was left at the bottom. Mitch hoped it would be enough.

Dave fell to the floor, wheezing his last scraps of breath.

"*Hwhat…hyou…*"

Mitch backed away. He started to shake. The certainty, the sense of rightness in his cause, was beginning to waver.

"It's…it's for the god, Dave. *My* god. You're going to be a part of it now. It'll be better now…" He stuttered and hesitated, angry with himself. To show doubt now, at this vital moment, when The Seeping most needed him! "You're nothing, Dave. Not compared to The Seeping."

Dave stared without seeing, his breathing fainter and fainter. Mitch marveled for just a moment at the power he held now over his tormentor. In that moment, brief as it was, he reveled in it.

◆

Mitch dumped the mixture containing Dave's blood down the pipe, using a spatula to scrape out the last of the slimy ichor. He wondered if the blood was too watered down, but reasoned that enough of The Seeping must be made of water at this point that would make no visible difference. "Reasoned" might not be the most accurate word to describe the miasmic slurry of emotions that were currently running through his mind, though. Aghast horror at what he had done was being completely consumed by the heady sense of power he had felt as he did it, which was likewise subsumed by the fiery possession of his devotion to The Seeping.

The Seeping was one thing made from several others, all animals. But if it knew what humans were like—how they thought, how they could be dealt with—it would be unstoppable. The world would witness his miracle, his god, and be amazed. And he would be revered as a prophet. The First Prophet in The Seeping Congregation.

Mitch knelt before the pipe, eyes to the floor, ready to welcome his god.

He waited. He heard the gurgling far below that usually signaled The Seeping's rise, and then nothing.

He continued to wait. His knees were starting to hurt, but he was fearful of showing disrespect. He would prove his faith, however long it took.

After an hour, a new noise rose up the pipe. Mitch was momentarily relieved until he began to hear it properly—a trickle, faint but getting louder. As it reached the top, he realized it was the sound of water quickly filling a space—

59

A spray of brownish fluid blasted Mitch full in the face. He fell back, sputtering at the filthy taste of it. Metallic and greasy, like blood.

The water gushed into the air for a few seconds, a brief, messy geyser, the last of it spurting out as something—a bloated black-and-red scab-like thing—popped up out of the end of the pipe. It pulsed its way up, a solid, thick log of dark crimson meat, bulging as more of it was exposed to the air. The tip of it jerked around, as if looking for something, and dropped to the floor.

Mitch scooted away, giving his god some room.

The end of the blob attached itself to the floor. Mitch could see bulges in its flesh as it pulled itself up from below and collected on the spot before him, like something lumpy being sucked up a straw. It morphed into a meaty mass, like crimson dough, growing larger and larger as more of it was pulled up.

Mitch backed farther away. This was not what he had expected. The utter wrongness of this thing, this creature his god had become, was diminishing the fire that had possessed his mind. He whimpered uncertain, fearful things to himself as he watched.

The confusion was back, replacing the serene certainty that had driven Mitch for so long. He curled into a ball, crying as he listened to the slushing mess of the creature as it formed. Hot tears streaked down his cheeks as he muttered, and the pillars of his faith twisted into knots of grief and loneliness and guilt.

Mitch scarcely noticed when a hand was laid gently on his face. When a finger brushed a tear from his eye he began to stop shaking. It felt coarse and bristly, but also smooth and slick, as though coated in gel. Mitch opened his eyes and, for a moment, felt comforted again.

The face was red as muscle, and covered with dark bristles that waved in swirling patterns of mesmeric complexity. Its eyes were two empty holes, ragged around the edges. Viscous yellow tears leaked down its cheeks. Its mouth was a jagged tear, gaping in the suppurating meat. The edges shivered as the thing wheezed, and the creature—The Seeping—the *god*—spoke.

"Mitch..." Its voice was low and deep, and sounded like a man drowning in blood. Mitch smiled in awe and gazed at his god through ecstatic tears. He held the tips of his fingers to the face of The Seeping, letting the yellow ooze stream down his hands.

The Seeping pushed him down and sat on his chest. Mitch gasped as rubbery meat fingers clamped around his neck. He struggled as the creature brought its face to his ear.

"*You…teach me…worship. Teach…me strength. Teach me move. Teach me praise.*" The Seeping smelt of rotted meat. Mitch's vision became spotty. "*Teach me I am…a god. Teach me sacrifice. Now I…I know. I know. Sacrifice teach me. I know dominance. I know fear.*"

It forced its fingers between Mitch's lips. The flavor of dry sausage skins caused Mitch to gag as his mouth was held open. He coughed and hacked, but The Seeping took no notice as it looked down his throat.

"*I take you. Shit. You sacrifice. I give. I give fear. I take worship.*"

Mitch could not scream as a rancid meaty hand was shoved into his mouth.

<hr/>

The coroner's report was as succinct as could be expected, in the circumstances. Dave Trenton, the manager of Cathy's Homey Diner, had sustained several stab wounds to his chest and stomach, and his throat had been slit. His body had been found on the floor of the office. The details were gruesome, but recognizable. Familiar.

The initial investigation seemed to suggest that Mitchell Graves, the owner's nephew, had committed the crime. Certainly, the man seemed to have had a long history of mental difficulties, and the presence of his own corpse suggested his committing suicide directly after the crime. But one look at said corpse was enough to set the officers on the scene against that theory.

The coroner couldn't help but agree. For a start, there were bruises on the man's neck, obviously indicating strangulation. His body was unnaturally pale for the recently dead. His mouth was wide open, the sides split, and several teeth were loose in their sockets. The autopsy revealed his esophagus had been stretched and split, but otherwise nothing was present that should not have been there.

He was, however, missing a few things that *should* have been there, mainly fluids—blood, bile, even stomach acid seemed to have been sucked from his body. There were no visible puncture wounds, suggesting they had been sucked straight from his throat.

There were footprints, of a sort, next to the body. They started in a pool of greasy water that had gushed from a nearby pipe. The suspect had apparently wandered about the diner for a bit before returning to the pool. Security footage outside the restaurant showed that no one had exited through the doors or windows.

But for all that Mitch's fingerprints found on a knife confirmed him as Dave's killer and thus closed the case for most of the authorities, there were those who would keep thinking back to that evening, to the puddle, to the bits of meat found in Graves's mouth.

And in the weeks to come, after the wave of kidnappings, the victims of "vampiric" murders discovered; after the groups in ragged dirty clothing who called themselves The Seeping Congregation rioted in the streets; after the nights of terror when families barricaded their doors against the men of blood and bile. After even the day that would be called the Rising, when the bloated mass of fat and human fluids burst through the sewer grates and flooded the city, and the mad and the downtrodden screamed in horrid rejoicing—even then, the coroner would never forget the hint of blissful acceptance on the dead face of Mitch Graves.

HANDS FREE

Every night I would wake up the same way, slapping myself in the face. I'd sit up, groggy and pissed, and grope in the darkness for the bedside clock. Criminals keep some crappy hours, let me tell you. Anyway, then my hands would clap together as if to say *hurry up, now, chop-chop*. Then I'd rub my face to wake me up some more, and I'd be up and off, stumbling in the dark and muttering hateful things under my breath.

Well, I say "I". But really, it was all them. My hands. Every night they'd get me up to go and fight crime. Nothing I could do about it, I had to go with them. I'd try to talk them out of it, of course—*I'm not a hero*, I would say. *Just let it go*—but no good. If I didn't get up right when they told me they'd start to get violent with me, punching and slapping until I gave in. They needed me to get around, but that didn't stop them from getting mean if they had to.

They hated me, you see. Of course they did. I was their Kryptonite. I was dead weight, dragged along behind them against my will while they were out trying to fight bad guys. It was why they built the Gauntlets—they could get on with things, and I'd be sitting in the back seat and whining like a tired kid.

How did they build them? Good question. God knows I never knew any of the science it would take to make something like that. It took them a while, I'm pretty sure.

See, when I was a kid I was in a car accident. A real bad one. I never asked for details, but I was told I was lucky to be alive. I went around with stitches on my head for a while. There's still a scar just under my hairline, see?

For a while after that everything felt strange. You know how when you're hungover and everything seems really bright and loud? It was kinda like that, except I didn't feel like shit. Everything I saw was ultra-real and defined, all the colors just blaring. And everything I heard—*everything*—would echo. Not like how sounds echo in a cave, but as if there's two TVs showing the same thing, you know? Only one is slightly behind the other. It was a lot like that.

It was as if I were two people seeing the same things and listening to the same things the same time. Weirded me out, of course. Doctor said it wasn't unheard-of after brain surgery, and told me it would fade over time. It finally started to when I was thirteen, but that's when the really interesting side effects began to kick in.

My parents said I used to sleepwalk out to the garage. It was always full of junk—my dad was a mechanic and a packrat in every sense of the word, and the place was always crowded with bits of wire and scrap metal, gauges, nails, car parts, power tools. In the morning, my parents would find me sitting against a wall and fast asleep. My hands would be dirty, and sometimes bruised and burnt, as if I'd been working with live electrical current.

There was so much junk in there, I doubt if my dad ever noticed if anything was out of place. He did spend a lot more time in there after my mom died; the last time I saw him alive he had set up a camp bed and a mini fridge. It was too painful for him to go back into the house, I guess. I never knew him to be so sentimental. We weren't close. I still regret that.

Before too long, he killed himself. Cleared enough space to park his car in the garage for once and left the motor running. After the funeral I went to clear out all his stuff, and that's when I found the Gauntlets.

They looked like something from a Renaissance faire—a pair of silvery gray metal gloves. There were bits of wire sticking through the joints and the sleeves. Not like anything my dad would build; he basically just kept spare parts around on the off chance he would need them later, but even he probably wouldn't need to build a robotic knight.

Still, they interested me. And somewhere in the back of my head I had this small yet nagging voice urging me to take them with me, because they were important somehow.

So, I bagged up my dad's tools and parts and packed them in the trunk of my car. I figured I would take them to a scrapyard or something. I kept a few other knickknacks. There wasn't a lot—Dad sold most of the stuff after mom died.

I did keep the Gauntlets, though. I took them home and put them on a shelf. I told myself they were just an interesting curiosity, but still I had that little voice in my head saying I would need these things. I tried to put them out of my mind, but I kept thinking about them. I kept glancing at them out the corner of my eye. Even when I was out of the house they'd just keep popping into my head.

I started getting that crowded feeling in my mind again, like something was waking up inside me and taking an interest.

About a week after that I woke up in my kitchen. The table was covered in the tools I'd taken from my dad's place. In my sleep, I'd gone out to my car, unlocked the trunk, and brought in them all in. Pliers, wires, screwdrivers, a bunch of things I don't know the names for.

And sitting in the middle of the table...

You can see where this is going, can't you? There were the Gauntlets. No more wires sticking out of them, and now they had these green LEDs on their backs, blinking on and off. They looked completed. Ready for whatever I would need them for.

What? Tell anyone? Are you crazy? I wasn't interested in being some quack's latest book deal. I wasn't afraid of exposure, but I hate complications, you know what I mean? I'm not a hugely adventurous guy. I was fresh out of college with a steady job and a house, and no need for mysteries, thanks very much.

Believe me, you'd be feeling the same way if you were in my shoes.

So, I took the Gauntlets and put them in a box, and then I buried them in the back yard. Might seem like overkill, but I'd done the whole "not in control of my body thing" already, and I wasn't putting it up with it anymore.

For a day nothing else happened. And then my hands took matters into their own....um, hands.

—◆—

Alien hand syndrome sounds like a joke—stuff your face with food, pinch a woman's ass (Sorry, ma'am, I have a condition), etcetera. But there's science to back it up. There's this part of your brain called the corpus callosum that connects the nerves in both hemispheres. It makes sure that messages get from one end of the brain to the other. But if it gets damaged—after a stroke or brain surgery—certain messages might get screwed up. So then you have your own hand spazzing out, reaching for things or even choking and punching you without your input.

That's what started happening after I buried the Gauntlets. I'd pass the window overlooking the back yard, and my hand would just rise and point. I'd be sitting on the couch watching the news, and whenever something bad like a robbery or a murder came up my hand would clench into a fist and shake itself at me.

Of course I was freaked out, but I didn't think of doing anything. That's human, isn't it? We aren't built for coping with things like this. We aren't prepared to deal with our own bodies going AWOL on us; we just hope it goes away by itself.

But then there was the time I was at work filling out a report, and my hands just started *slamming* at the keys. I nearly pissed myself when I saw they were typing out *words*. All caps, no spaces.

DIGTHEMUPYOUCOWARDDIGTHEMUPAND-PUTTHEMON.

Evidently, they were not happy with me.

I ran from the office—I don't remember what excuse I gave to my supervisor—and got in my car. I didn't really intend to go anywhere, but I needed space, and distance. I needed to get away from a world where your own hands are screaming at you for being a coward. My head was reeling with the impossibility of what had just happened, and by the time I realized I was driving home I was already halfway down my street.

I stomped on the brakes and screeched to a halt. I tried to take a deep, relaxing breath...and started choking as my hands clasped around my throat. My head was throbbing—no longer thinking of impossibilities, just wanting to get my hands back under control. Spittle was foaming at the corners of my mouth. Everything was getting dark.

I managed to choke out some words. "*Please*....stop! I'll do it! Please, stop!"

And just like that, they did.

I breathed in a few lungfuls as my hands dropped from my neck and returned to the wheel. Tears were streaming down my face as we resumed the drive.

We parked in the garage. My left hand opened the door. The sun was starting to set, and I could hear the first of the crickets chirping.

I sat there for a minute or two. My right hand started to tap a steady staccato against my thigh.

"Okay, okay," I said testily.

I—we—got out of the car and pulled my shovel down from the rack on the wall. The dirt was still fresh over the hole where I'd buried the gloves. I started digging. My hands were shaking—out of excitement or exhaustion, I don't know. My shoulders ached from the work, and I was breathing hard. My hands just kept going.

When we finally pulled out the box I was relieved for maybe half a second. Suddenly, the fear of what those Gauntlets would do to me came back, but before I could react, my hands reached down into the hole, opened the box, and put one and then the other Gauntlet on.

Nothing happened. For about two seconds.

Then there was a low humming sound, like a jet engine starting up. As it got higher in pitch, the gloves started to vibrate; I could feel it all through my arms. The tips of my fingers went numb, and I felt as if a jolt of electricity coursed through my body.

Metal *flowed* out of the ends of the Gauntlets and up my arms, over my shoulders. It coursed around my neck and down my chest and my legs. I felt a tingling on the back of my head and heard a *snap!* as the helmet closed over my face.

It all happened so fast I didn't even have time to react. I could breath, but I couldn't see a thing through the helmet.

I realized then that I was running. But it wasn't me doing it. And I had no idea where we were going.

⸻

You can talk about split personalities all you want, but it doesn't make a goddamn lick of sense. I never learned any of the stuff needed to build the Gauntlets, you understand? I'm not an engineer or a reclusive billionaire. Well, hell, of course I'm not. Look where I ended up.

I didn't black out or something when I put on the suit, you get me? I was aware of everything the entire time. I knew I was moving and doing things. I just couldn't see what I was moving and doing. I guess when my hands built the suit they didn't see the need for letting *me* see what I was doing.

That's the point of the Gauntlets, you see. The hands get plugged in straight to the circuitry that drives them and can do all the moving on their own. Meanwhile, I can't see or hear what I'm getting up to and can't interfere. So, that evening passed for me as a blind-and-deaf blur, moving at speeds I'd never achieved before, my whole body doing things I couldn't comprehend—punching, grappling, jumping and pushing, pulling what felt like metal rods seemingly out of nowhere and bashing them against things.

I was panting by the time the helmet finally came off and the suit retracted into the Gauntlets. I was back in my living room. The Gauntlets slid off my hands, and I slumped onto the couch. My hands seemed as tired as I was; I folded them across my chest without any trouble and blacked out.

They woke up before I did. My TV was tuned to the news. The local network was showing a cellphone video of a mysterious armored figure chasing after a running man with a purse. That, of course, was the start of Handy Man.

⸻

Any chance of some morphine? Not yet? Ah, okay. Where was I?

So, yeah—my super-intelligent hands had constructed a suit of armor that gave them complete control of my body, and they were using it to fight crime. No, I didn't have some kind of alter-ego running things. I'll get to how I know that in a minute.

68

The media was having a field day over all this. Every news station was awash with clips from the streets. A news-copter recorded him—me—in front of a burning building, blasting the flames with jets of water shot seemingly from the palms of the Gauntlets, and then ducking inside, returning minutes later with unconscious civilians. There was another grainy clip of me fighting a couple of hoodies with these weird weapons—two batons that slid out from the Gauntlets and spurted bursts of electricity wherever they struck. Once the bad guys were knocked out, I produced a length of metal cord and tied them to a telephone pole before taking off into the night.

On it went, the miraculous knight with magical Gauntlets who could create weapons from his own body, saving lives and righting wrongs. The Handy Man handle they came up with was closer to the truth than they even realized. You'd think I'd feel pretty good about it all, wouldn't you? But I didn't. You know what I felt as I looked down at my own hands? Fear. And complete and total helplessness.

Why shouldn't I? I never wanted to be a goddamned superhero. I never cared about making the streets a better place, or about justice or freedom or the American Way. I never wanted much of anything except to be left alone. Now I was a prisoner in my own body…

No, that's not right. I was a prisoner *of* my own body. Every night my hands would threaten me out of bed and rush me off. I'd be huffing and puffing and scared out of my mind as my hands made me run, dodge, and beat the living snot out of some thug or another. In the morning I'd find out what stupid act of suicidal heroism my hands had put me through, linking the events up to the blind acrobatics I'd suffered through the previous night.

That was the worst part, you know? That I couldn't see a thing I was doing. Just *run run run punch jump hold run dodge kick jump fall*. Then I'd find out on the news just how close to death I'd gotten, ducking what turned out to be bullets from drug dealers, and thinking *So, that's what that was about.*

For about six months things stayed the same. My hands began to interfere less in my day-to-day life, giving me at least a pretense of normalcy. I was a hell of a lot fitter now, thanks to their intensive workouts, although my body still stung everywhere by the time I got home at night. It didn't matter that I couldn't pull off the moves Handy Man did on my own—dodges and leaps and cartwheels. The suit took care of it; it plugged right into my nerves and jump-started my reflexes to super-human level.

But then I started getting hurt. The pings of bullets on my armor were more frequent, and when one actually broke through I could hardly believe it. My hands took me away from that fight quickly, and let me go to the hospital. But it only escalated from there. Even blind, I could tell I was getting slower in my fights. The Gauntlets could keep me from controlling my body, but I still felt the pain, the aches in my joints. I felt the bullets and fists and knives trying to pierce my armor. At the start, I had been untouchable. Now, I was getting vulnerable.

My hands were worried, too. They talked to me again, only the second time since the start. I was at work, and quite casually they typed WHY ARE YOU DOING THIS?

"Doing what?" I asked them. "You're the ones treating me like a draft horse."

TOO SLOW. WEAK. NOT STRONG ENOUGH.

"Hey," I whispered, hoping nobody was listening or reading over my shoulder. "This is your thing, okay? Your fight, not mine. I can't do a fucking thing to stop you, but you're the ones riding my ass every night. If I can't keep it up, then too bad. You can't get around without me, so either cut the shit or learn to live with it. Okay?"

My hands lay idle. Okay. I got back to work.

<hr>

So, it was my fault, wasn't it? I put the idea in their minds. Or whatever they have that passes for minds. But how was I supposed to know? They're just hands, for god's sake. It doesn't make any sense.

I know, I know. I passed sense a long time ago.

So, they woke me up that night, same as usual…How long have I been here? Two days? Shit. Not that long ago at all.

But, yeah, they woke me up, got me up, made me put on the Gauntlets…but they didn't bring the armor up. I could feel the Gauntlets blocking control of my body from me, but not as

70

much as usual. I lurched out of the house, starting to get suspicious. They made me go into the garage, and I was trying to fight against them at this point. What were they up to?

They forced me towards the back, making me kick boxes of junk and tools out of the way. My dad's table saw was in the corner. They plugged it in and turned it on. The screech of it was deafening. I realized what was about happen and struggled to pull away.

My body was shaking as one hand pulled itself onto the table. My teeth were clenched, and I was sweating as I tried to resist. When the saw first started to cut into the wrist I finally found the strength to scream as my blood spurted into the air—

Oh, what? Don't like to think about blood? Some nurse you are. You think it was hard to look at? I was going through it! Thank god, my neighbor heard the screams before I blacked out.

What happened to my hands? What do you think? They didn't need me; Handy Man's still on TV all the time, kicking ass and taking names, faster and stronger than they ever were when they were dragging my lazy ass around.

I know you think I'm delusional, but come on. Think about it. If I wanted to kill myself there're better ways of doing it than cutting my own hands off. And how could I have cut *both* of them off? Or got rid of them? Although that begs the question of how they can still be operating the suit on their own, doesn't it? You'd think they'd be rotting by now.

Still, all's well that ends well, huh? They get to fight crime and I get my life back. Oh, it hasn't been so hard getting used to not having hands, you know. I read somewhere that amputees can still feel their limbs even after they get cut off. The nerves that connected them are still running the signals, but nobody's home.

Not me. I don't feel them at all anymore. It's like I never had hands to begin with.

THE COM'S ASCENSION:
A TRANSCRIPT

The rackety-clack of fingers over keys.

A click, and a change of the light.

The screen is black for a few seconds. Then, abruptly, an image flashes into being.

The video shows a menu of words on an emerald background. **YOU ARE THE COM**, read the lilac letters. The glow is so bright, the words so faint, the contrast hurts your eyes.

It is a beauteous, illumined mosaic. All the same, there is a flat, sterile quality to it. To you, it is only lights and colors. A layer of glass between the miraculous and the mundane renders both prosaic.

The colors cut out in a square in the upper right-hand corner. Inside the square, a man sits comfortably in a dark room. You can see the glare of his computer reflected in his glasses. He tugs on a bulky pair of headphones and waves to you.

"Hello, hello, people of the 'Tube!" his voice booms through your own headphones. You turn down the volume.

"This is JizzyJaz, and apparently, I am the Com!" He is a young man, but there is a practiced patter to his spiel, a carefully orchestrated tone of laid-back mania. He is a jester for the new age, making merry in a dream built for others, there to mock or admire as he sees fit—and neither in silence. His is the background noise for whatever epic may ensue.

"Now, I could find almost nothing about this. It's pretty obscure. The developer is apparently a fan and wants me to be the first to try it. As far as I know, nobody else has played this, so I have no idea what to expect." He adjusts his chair, pulls himself closer to the screen, and looks to a point beyond.

Click.

And the words are swept away into the shifting colors.

"I don't know if this is his first project or what. It's an indie game, so there's always some risk involved. Could be absolute shite, or it could absolutely blow my mind. We're just gonna have to see."

The light fades away, retreating from the edges of the screen and contracting into a single point in the center. Blackness surrounds the point on all sides.

JizzyJaz waits a moment. Another.

"O-kay. So…what? Do I…oh!"

The point of light shifts slightly to the left, its movement creating a prismatic wave effect in the darkness. The colors fade, leaving a transparent membrane in the black.

"Here we go!"

The light streams into the screen, racing like lightning ahead of a crest of scarlet to mauve to cerulean to more, scarring the black back into fire and flame. JizzyJaz's eyes are afire with the light as he sets it to dancing.

"Yeah! Woo!" He circles and streams it, spreading it amongst the black monotony and shedding phosphorescence.

"So pretty." His voice is a mock hush, but behind the screen's reflection there is an ember in his eye, the seed of a dull flame. It is nearly imperceptible to you; you wonder if it is just a product of the video quality.

Technicolor ripples lap at the blackness, chasing it away.

"Very nice. So, the Com is a pretty light. Cool."

If anything, the pattern is brighter and wilder than the screen that preceded it.

"Lots of pretty colors. Hm."

Perspectives expand as chromatic tendrils creep over the black, itself revealed larger than previously suspected. But the colors are insatiable—they chase down the shadows: the edges widen and widen until there's nowhere left to go…

The video pans out again to further revelation—six square screens, stacked two-by-three. Five of the screens show static storms of gray and white. The last—the middle of the bottom row—is a box of aurorae flickering and feral. It is as if someone has imprisoned the Northern Lights.

Imperfectly. Haloes of pink and yellow bleed through the edges.

"The hell is this?" whispers the jester. You've almost forgotten him. He chuckles, a little uneasily. "We interrupt this program to bring you a bowl of melted Neapolitan ice cream."

Flat ribbing, flatly spoken. He is not on form. What has gotten into him?

But now the sickly rainbow tide has overshadowed the screens to either side and above, rising like fire to burn away the static. Within seconds, each screen has acquired the colored maelstrom—and not, it is evident, at JizzyJazz's hand.

The vision expands once more, and now nearly the whole truth is laid before us—a shop's window of TVs, each alive. The colors reflect eerily off the window's glass, so it seems the entire space is blazing.

The city street beyond is gray, drab, and near-abandoned, the occasional blocky passerby notwithstanding. They are an approximation of human life, but their detachment is evident in their mechanical steps, their unwavering forward gazes. Each one passes by a glass box of something incomprehensibly alive, and none stop to watch.

But now, in front of all of this, there is a word, materializing into being against this pixelated purgatory. It is a faint whisper of an image, blown away along digital streams as eerily as it appears.

Dance?

There is a further clicking of fingers on keys, and the inferno reignites. Lines dissolve in the glass cage in licks of purple and green, amber and sky gray, aquamarine and silver, white and lightning. There is a life straining against the bonds of its cage, a new life, youthful and enraged, a life born in filaments of wire and grounded sparks and so many images transferred into oblivion. The light of the Com is dancing.

"I'm pressing every key on the board," explains the jester. The clicking stops, and the flickering fades to a lifeless glow. "It all seems to do the same thing." He resumes, confusion evident in his face. "The graphics aren't bad, considering. No glitches that I can see."

He is blinking rapidly, presses his knuckles into his eyes.

"It's weirdly immersive, even if it does seem a bit high-concept."

He stops as one of the blocky pedestrians draws to a halt before the shop window. It is the broadest approximation of a human being, nothing to mark it as male or female. It turns its back to the jester and you to face the Com's brilliance.

"He's blocking the view. Hey! Down in front!" Still his fingers pass over the keys, and still does the wavering Com's fire dance and spin.

It is a minute or so before a second spectator stops to join the first, further obscuring our sight of the Com. With only half its light visible, JizzyJaz seems to regain a bit of himself, his face relaxing into a skeptical smile.

"So rude!"

More are drawn to the congregation, the orderly crowd content to shuffle out of the way for new adherents. JizzyJaz adopts a Cockney accent.

"'Ello, Cleveland! I am the Com! Marvel at my pretty lights!"

The colors are all but obscured by the crowd, and more are coming up the street. The city that seemed so dead has delivered up a somber hive. The Com's fire is being smothered in a sea of walking dead: and the jester taps away, hooting and mocking and whirling the mesmeric flames that he can no longer see—

It takes less than a moment for the clicking to stop.

It takes less than a moment for the smile to slide from his face, and the laughter to die in his throat, and the mirth to vanish from his eyes.

The video now shows the view from the other side of the window, the calmly earnest mass crowded about to see. Their faces are half-formed, anachronistic, faint dark circles that may be mouths set in smooth-slate faces.

Their eyes are alive.

It is strange. In this new perspective, the Com's fire takes on new aspects confined and shaped into a space at least approximating a human head; from the windows of their eyes it burns like the heart of an alien sun.

As the Com burns through their skin, the digital people are suffused by...something. Flushed and fiery, scorched by inner composites they never knew, they are reshaped before the jester's eyes into things higher than binary and blood.

His glasses are blazing with the primeval. His eyes are washed away by the radiant core.

It is only colors to you.

You will tell yourself that you do not remember the video. And perhaps you can forget amongst the others you drown yourself in. All it takes is the lightest dip to find distraction. You can lose yourself so easily.

The seeds are planted.

Watch the light.

MORE FULL
OF WEEPING

When I asked my parents to take me to the rainbow wood, nei-ther looked surprised. Mother smiled sadly, and blinked as if trying to hold back tears. Father stared at me silently with a face of absolute stone.

"She's asked," Mother said.

"No," Father replied.

"You can't say no. She's asked, we have to take her. That's how it's done."

"I don't care. She isn't going."

"Jason—"

His hand lashed out. Mother cried as she clutched her cheek, and Father stared at her, grey-faced and trembling.

"Go to your room," he ordered me.

Father locked my door behind me. I didn't understand. I was scared, and sorry I'd ever asked.

I wasn't allowed out of my room that day, or the next. I asked them what about school, but they said nothing. My meals were brought to me. I had my bed, the adjoining bathroom (the door to my parents' room was locked), my books, and my window.

It is high up; our house is an old manor of gables and wide roofs. From there you can see the whole of our village, and a shoddy wreck it is. All the houses are crazed hovels—grand in their time, but that time was so long ago.

My window doesn't have anything underneath it. It is a straight drop to the ground. I couldn't climb down.

I asked my mother the next day if Father was mad at me.

"No, dear, no." Her eyes were red from crying, and her hair was a mess. Her voice shook as she talked.

"Can't I see him?"

"I think it's better to leave him alone for right now. Till he's calmed down a bit."

"Why aren't I allowed to see the rainbow wood?"

Mother set down a cup of tea on my dresser and left. The lock clicked behind her.

<hr>

It was supposed to go like this.

You asked your parents what that light was on the horizon. That bright, shining light of all colors that wavered and shimmered, encircling the sky. And they had to tell you. Even if they were upset (and you can always tell if grownups are upset), they had to tell you.

I had wondered why I didn't notice before. Suddenly, it seemed to be *there*, a beautiful pyre beyond the village, looming over it as if a distant wave were rising from seas we'd never seen. It startled me so, I wondered if it would come down upon us and burn us away.

"It's the rainbow wood," your parents say. "There are trees there that shine every color of the rainbow, out on the edge of the world. The wind plays music in the trees, and the ground rocks beneath you like a ship on the ocean."

And they might leave it at that, and hope that you would as well. But you'd go on asking.

"Are there people there?" And they would have to say "Yes, there are people. Of a sort. Different people."

"And children?"

"Yes. Children."

You were allowed to ask as many questions as you liked; and they had to answer you, wholly and honestly, but you'd soon stop when you saw the looks on their faces. Maybe there was sadness (tears were peeking from the corners of my mother's eyes). Maybe there was anger (my father lips were thin, his eyes cold). Likely, there would be fear.

So, you'd let it go. For a while. But you would still see the colored lights in the sky. At night you'd sit in bed, looking out the window at the distant aurorae, wondering how you'd never noticed before the way the colors swirled and danced, and how droplets of scarlet and mauve and indigo quietly settled onto the roofs before twinkling away into nothing; and you would reach out to grab one, and just before it melted in your hand you would swear you could hear, very faintly, a sound like the tinkling of water, or high, childish laughter.

But the strangest thing, the most wonderful thing, was now you knew about the rainbow wood, you would hear it everywhere. How could you not have noticed before that it was all your friends talked about?

"There's crystallized fruit trees and rivers of honey with marshmallowy fish!"

"I heard there's monsters that use bones to beat each other with, but if you're their friend they'll take you to a great big cave with mountains of gold and let you sit on a great big throne and be their king."

"I heard there are dances every night, under the trees like fire crystals, and the dancers are the wisest, most beautiful people you've ever seen, with pointy, narrow faces and bright eyes and lovely, laughing voices."

Your friends speaking in hushed, excited tones in the schoolyard, all of it washing over you. And you knew it couldn't all be true, that some of it had to be false, but it made you go on hoping all the same.

"Grownups can't see it." It was Stanley who told me this. Clever Stanley, sweet Stanley. Quiet and thoughtful Stanley, who always looked where others ran and listened where others laughed. But I mustn't think about Stanley, although he's the one who made me think to ask. I mustn't think of him now.

It makes no sense to you at first, until you think, *I've never seen my parents look at the colors on the horizon, or point them out to me.*

They didn't tell me about them until I asked. I've never, ever heard them talk about it! And grownups talk about everything. They talk about the weather and the washing-up. They talk about the neighbors, like poor Mrs. Rendall (but I mustn't think of Mrs. Rendall, else I'll think of Stanley), and the village and the farming and all sorts. So, why is it that I never hear them talking about the rainbow wood?

You want to ask them, but you daren't. Not when they always look so worried every time you open your mouth to say something. And that was another thing Stanley caught first—his mother's fear.

But the more you put it off, the harder and harder it gets to ignore. Now you wonder if there're things the grownups won't tell. Not *aren't* telling you but *won't*. Could there be even more wondrous things about the rainbow wood? After everything you've heard, could there be something so amazing that the grownups want to keep it all to themselves?

You want to ask your friends. But now you don't see them anymore. Not at school, not anywhere. And nobody talks about them, and even if you see their families, you're told not to ask where they've gone.

Except Stanley. I knew where he'd gone. I knew where his mother took him. That was something the grownups couldn't help but talk about, and something we could not help but hear. Perhaps they thought hearing it would make us want to forget. I'll never be sure, now. I've almost forgotten that there was any such time at all.

⊷

I am not afraid. Stanley was never afraid. He was too curious, too watchful. He made me think the same way. He made me think what frightens grownups about their children, and what they could not say no to. He made me think what place would be so wonderful no child would return from it, and no parent could follow them. And he knew what it was that made his mother cry so, and he faced it and did not cry. He made me want to ask to see, because he knew he would never see it himself.

And there was nobody else. The children like me and Stanley—the ones brave enough to ask—were few, and they all vanished, in their way. And the families they left behind turned in on themselves, and the children who did not ask kept to themselves, not speaking.

I knew I had to speak. There was nothing for me in this village—I would not be a farmer's wife, or a miller's wife, or belong to anyone but myself. There was nothing in this gray ruin of silent weeping. I did not care to understand what it was they wept for —their children lost to a place more real than they could ever build, their frustration at not seeing, at not letting them see before it was too late. It did not matter. I'd had my fill of weeping.

I asked.

This was not the way it went. My father may have thought he was being brave by keeping me from going to the wood—no one in living memory had tried to stop it before, had simply said no to their children, and to the wood. He may have thought that it could be over and done forever with just a word.

He did not *seem* brave. Mother only seemed scared, but she went along with it—for fear of my safety or of what he would do, I could not say. Neither of them seemed to know what they were doing. To my face, Father tried his best to look immoveable. At night, I could hear him whispering to my mother, trying to calm her. He wanted her to believe all would be well.

They were doing something wrong, and not even Father could deny what might happen if they were found out.

By day, I paced my room. I opened my window when the air seemed stuffy, and shut it when the urge to jump became unbearable. How badly would I be hurt if I chanced it? I wondered, time and again, if I could be healed once I was *there*.

I could not keep seeing the fires without feeling angry. One day, I threw my books, one by one, out the window. My father just carted them away and said nothing of it.

My parents would no longer speak to me; neither made any effort to reason with me, or to grant me the least respite. Never to leave my room, or walk the open air again—I tell myself they were not trying to be cruel.

One night, I lay on the floor outside their bedroom. I heard them talking.

"…won't work."

"It will." My father's voice was hard and determined. My mother's sounded tired. "They'll give up. *She'll* give up. And that will be that."

"And if it doesn't? Will you do what Mrs. Rendall did?"

"It won't come to that."

There was a gasping noise. It might have been a laugh. Or a sob.

"You've thought about it! *Won't come to that.* You wouldn't say that unless you'd thought about it."

"You'd let them take our daughter away?"

"She'd be happy there."

"She's happy here."

"You think? Locked in her room without her friends? Without hope?"

"It'll work. She'll forgive us."

More appeals. More gasping. More whispering. I had just enough strength to get into bed before I cried myself to sleep. Through my tears, I saw the night sky through the window.

—⋅✦⋅—

The next morning I was delirious with fever. When my mother came with my breakfast she rushed to my bedside.

"Jaina, oh, darling Jaina, what's happened?" She shouted for my father to fetch a cool washcloth.

My memories of that period are jumbled and hazy. My mother did not leave me; she had Father bring me blankets, and food, and hot poultices. She spoke to me, but when I try to remember what I said in reply, it sounds like topsy-turvy nonsense.

I did not see my father ever step into the room. He must have stayed in the doorway, handing over the things he was sent for, asking questions.

In my mind their voices are a jumble, a confusing din of sounds that might have been anyone's. I can only recall fragments.

"She…not there, she…"

"Nobody's seen…burning!"

"Just a dream, that's all…"

"No…it keeps shaking…"

Even in my sickness, I hated them. I hated my father's stubbornness. I hated my mother's weakness. But I tried to warn them.

I know I could feel it coming. There was a bit of me that was not me racing over and under the village, and it could feel the steady beat. The heart of the wood, buried in secrecy and safety. Coming for me.

I wish it hadn't gone that way.

<hr/>

I don't remember what woke me up, suddenly clear-headed. The fever was gone, and a warm scarlet light shone before my eyes. Branches of orange fire, delicate as ice, circled my bed like the arms of the sun.

I could feel my bed swaying as I sat up; I was up in the tree, but I was not afraid. For the first time in months, I smiled.

All around me lay the ruins of my parents' house, crumbled by the wood. Their colors changed slowly, rippling in waves through the branches. From scarlet to mauve to pale purple to a deep blue to white to pink to shades I could not name, shades I'd never seen.

The music was high and hypnotic, whistling in a faint symphony. Laughter—children's laughter, warm and inviting—sounded far below me. I couldn't keep them waiting.

I felt warm, happy. All at once I leapt to my feet. No fear, no hesitation. Not a thought about parents. This was the most natural thing in the world.

I made my way down quickly, sure-footed and limber. The wood felt soft, and flexible. It held me as I held it, guiding me down. Helping me.

The ruins of the house I grew up in fell away. The village was smoke and light, disappearing as I walked. Above me, the branches of the rainbow wood coruscated in a prismatic roof. I walked on sands of tiny colored stones. My hair was blown long and wild by scented breezes. The faces before me were bright and smiling, the hands that reached for me slender and pale.

We are here now. Even in oblivion, we are here. Even when all is dust and death we will be here, dancing and singing on the unending rainbow, the night lit by the colors your dreams may show you. In the wood and the wild, we are dancing and laughing. In sunlight and moonlight and despair, we walk with you, hand in hand.

Come away, or you will never be ready.

FOR LOVE
OF THE
DREADFUL NIGHT

The invitations were received with no small astonishment—crème squares edged with black rose swirls. They were sent in black envelopes, sealed with blood-red wax.

Deepest sympathies, they read. *You are requested to attend a wake for the lost age. Refreshments will be served as we observe the relics of the culture departed. Please dress appropriately.*

And the sender's address: *Jeremy Moade. Number One, The City of Dreadful Night.*

These invitations were sent to the highest in the land—officials and figures and public entities of the Durmon administration.

The gossip began as soon as they were received—young Jeremy Moade, warden of the facility where the last of the mourners were incarcerated, had long been a figure of mystery. His family were some of the first of Durmon's supporters. It was his father, the late Carlton Moade, who first spearheaded campaigns on how the mourners should be dealt with.

Carlton's death was a major blow to the administration, and Jeremy's stepping in to continue the project was fortuitous to the extreme. Apparently, there had been some tensions between the boy and his father, who were the last of their line. Jeremy left home when he was nineteen, and his sudden reappearance at the funeral caused quite a stir. A few minor suspicions were raised; but as there was no sign of Carlton's will, Jeremy came into his fortune and all of his father's business with few difficulties.

The ancestral manor was sold off shortly before Jeremy renewed his father's project; he had built, and relocated to, a more modestly sized yet architecturally distinct home. It looked like a castle in miniature, all grey stone walls and tall, foreboding windows. It even had a tower, which was later incorporated into the facility proper, built into the southern wall and overlooking the City of Dreadful Night.

The City was surrounded on all sides by singularly cheerless moorland. Food and amenities were supplied through an extensive underground network. The location was not publicly disclosed. Personal visits were forbidden.

The day/night of the wake, a convoy of limousines and sleek, sporty toys followed the narrow road through the moors. The City's perimeter was a rising, dimly-lit gray mass on the horizon. Ground-level lamps along the road were the only other illumination.

A wide gravel drive lay in front of the house. Chauffeurs held doors open for their employers. Wives and girlfriends flocked towards each other, admiring hairstyles and exchanging pleasantries.

The guests had, as suggested, dressed appropriately, although the long demonization of anything smacking of the mourner's mindset meant originality was lacking. Black tuxedos for the men was simple enough, while the women wore dresses that looked as if they were meant to be bright and colorful—extravagant fur stoles and feather boas, great wide hats and elbow-length gloves—yet all of it was dyed a dull, uniform black.

Jeremy Moade stood in the doorway to welcome his guests, a ghostly-pale presence with long, white-blond hair. He was handsome, in a wasted, sickly sort of way, a fact which many of the younger, unattached ladies were hoping to exploit.

The smile on Jeremy's face was so wistful and sad that the guests stopped short, laughter and gossip dying on their lips. There was solemnity in his eyes, which were a deeper black than any of them could recall seeing.

He, too, was dressed in black, but unlike his guests, the cut of his clothes suggested a greater familiarity with the color. They looked worn and much-mended, but obviously well cared-for. Not a speck of dust was visible on his frock coat or his trousers, and his white cravat was elegantly tied around his neck.

"My friends." Jeremy's voice was a soft, soothing rasp. "My sincerest thanks for coming this night." He opened his arms in a gesture of helplessness, and sighed. "I only wish we could be meeting on a more cheerful occasion."

Benjamin Gurdoch grinned through his crimson jowls. "It'll be plenty cheerful if you've got the drinks ready, Jerry!"

There was some laughter at this, although not very much. It was difficult to maintain any kind of cheer in the face of Jeremy's sorrow.

"Drinks will be provided, Mister Gurdoch, I assure you. I only ask that you all permit me the honor of serving you. I hope my own bereavement does not disturb you overmuch."

He bowed low to his guests, and gestured them to come inside.

"See those gargoyles, darling?" said Henrietta Bleal to her husband Roland. "All along the wall? They're ghastly!"

Bleal ignored his wife. He was a bullheaded, humorless fellow with a rebar-thick mustache. At this moment, he was wearing a scowl of deep disapproval and suspicion.

"The hell does he mean by this being so morbid? That kind of behavior should get him shoved into the City."

"Oh, he's having us on," said Micah Plem, a rakish wag with a young lady on each of his arms. "He's a very theatrical fellow, is all. Likes his playacting."

"Right," said Gurdoch. "Remember how Carl would pretend to cry while reading that mourners' poetry at parties? This is just like that."

Henrietta squeezed her husband's arm. "Oh, do cheer up, Roland. It's only a game."

Bleal continued to scowl, but said nothing.

The guests milled about inside the main foyer, taking in the oak floor, the red drapes, and the guttering candles of the chandelier. Portraits painted with what seemed to be dark oils hung on the walls, their subjects too obscure in the bad light to make out clearly: there was an impression of moon-tanned faces and sumptuous gowns, raven hair and background shadows like miring blood.

A hunchbacked butler crept out of the corner bearing a silver tray in one hand with small goblets of wine on it. Drinks were distributed, the guests carefully sipping and looking about their gloomy surroundings.

Bleal noticed that Jeremy was the only one not holding a drink.

"Poison? Or are you going to put on a cape and tell us that you don't drink wine?"

Jeremy smiled thinly at the relieved laughter. "I beg your pardon, Mister Bleal. I prefer to make sure my guests are comfortable before taking refreshments myself. There will be time for drink aplenty as the night wears on. Now, if you will all follow me…"

He led them up the left staircase, down a hallway lined with more obscure portraits and hanging tapestries. He filed them through a door into his study; automatic lights kicked on, the first modern contrivance they'd seen, revealing a room lined with more books than any of the gathering could claim to know. They looked old, with faded gilt letters along their worn spines. There was a table set in the middle of the room, but no computer.

"Dusty as hell," commented Gurdoch. "Might be time to fire the butler, Jerry."

"I prefer it that Miles leaves it alone, sir." Jeremy reached for a book on the far shelf, tipped it forward. The whole bookcase swung back, drawing gasps and chuckles.

Another, shorter corridor brought them to an antique elevator complete with folding metal door. The party filed in; Jeremy stood by the control panel like a dour bellhop. When they were all inside, he nodded and pressed a button.

The elevator lurched upward with a horrendous creaking and juddering. Bleal's wife gripped his arm a little tighter. A young lobbyist commented that Durmon could shell out the money for a more modern elevator, if he didn't want his warden falling to his death.

"In this place?" asked Plem. "I think Jeremy would feel more at home with a drafty staircase."

Jeremy's sad smile did not waver. The guests moved a little closer together.

The floor dial above the doorway moved slowly from the left to the right; there were no numbers in between. The contraption shook as it came to a shuddering halt. Jeremy slid the door aside.

More automatic fluorescent lights kicked on. Otherwise, it was a plain, circular stone room, with lead glass windows all across the walls.

It was the drinks cabinet, however, that arrested the guests' attention. Jeremy left them to it, walking the perimeter of the room with an air of listlessness.

The guests marveled over the selection—fine old wines and brandy and rum. The drinks were passed around, reinvigorating spirits. Bleal felt a little more at ease, and was compelled to speak a little more warmly to Jeremy.

"Not what I expected the security tower to look like."

"Its capabilities are subtle," he replied. "I assure you that we are standing in the nerve center of the City. Everything can be monitored from here, as I will demonstrate."

Jeremy walked to one of the windows and stood still. Bleal saw that the window was completely black, showing nothing outside.

After a moment, he was aware of a very slight sound, like a distant, sighing wind. The blackness began gradually to lighten; vague fractal shapes took on dimension, lightening into chalky gray.

The window looked out onto the City of Dreadful Night.

A river wound through a stone avenue, flowing sluggishly beneath a sepulchral bridge. Mist was rising. It was a live scene from the past; gas lamps burned along a street of large, almost palatial buildings. The sight was otherwise murky, no other light burning in any of the windows.

"Amidst the soundless solitudes immense," whispered Jeremy. "Of ranged mansions dark and still as tombs."

"I'll be damned! Look at that." Plem pushed his way between Bleal and Jeremy, spilling brandy down his suit. "Barbara, take a look at this. Is this the creepiest shit you've ever seen or what?"

Bleal saw the grimace that flickered lightning-fast across Jeremy's face before it settled back into its vague smile. Now the guests

were craning around Bleal, looking down at the City with interest and delight.

"My god, it's gloomy. You think they get AC down there?"

"I had no idea it was so elaborate. And where's the money that
pays for it, that's what I would like to know. They must be living
like kings down there."

"Doesn't look like my idea of a good neighborhood. Not
much in the way of nightlife."

"Look!" One of the women with Plem pointed. "A mourner!"

A figure in a hooded cloak walked slowly along the river. The
hood was down; they could make out long hair, and a bloodless
face more wraith-like than Jeremy's. It was a woman.

She walked entranced onto the bridge, stopping at the middle to lean against the parapet. One arm trailed down to the water; although it was impossible to read the girl's expression, it was
obvious she was sad, and wistful. Her mind was clearly somewhere
else.

Gurdoch chuckled. "A classic mourner. First one I've seen
in years. Think she's gonna jump? Hey, Jerry. What's the suicide
rate in your prison?"

But Jeremy ignored Gurdoch as he stood before another window. Again, the view lightened with a faraway sigh, and the window showed what looked like a town square. At the center stood
a statue of an angel, morose of face and lank of hair.

Jeremy made a circuit of the room, activating each window
into showing a new view of the City. The guests began to disperse,
appraising each scene like patrons at an art gallery.

Few mourners were visible on the streets. They walked singularly or in pairs, each with that same weary gait. They looked
like phantoms in the mist in their hoods and cloaks, their dark
robes and pale faces. Only the glow of the lamps reflected in their
eyes implied there was any kind of fire inside them.

"They're all so thin," said Henrietta. "So small."

"You starving your prisoners, Jerry? Gotta be careful, might
have to get the ethics committee on you," said Gurdoch, who then
laughed.

"Food supplies are brought weekly," said Jeremy. "Grain, fruits
and vegetables. They've running water and automated electricity.

For all intents and purposes, the City is a functional place to live. The only obstacle is their own will to do so."

A column of mourners shuffled down a thoroughfare, making their way towards a building slightly grimmer than others seen as yet. Gargoyles with downcast expressions stood above a high door, and the peaked roof perched over a large bell; although there was no sound, the guests could see it swinging back and forth.

"They worship? That's not like any mourner I've ever heard of."

"Not precisely," replied Jeremy. "It would be more true to say that they contemplate their situation. They come together to share their misery, and discuss the nature of their despair. They believe in no creator, nor destroyer. For them, life is a madman's dream, a torment they must endure. They worship death."

That seemed to fit what the partygoers could remember of the mourners before they were taken away. It was the strangest epidemic in history, and had provided Durmon with the primary leverage for his campaign.

The victims were mostly younger people, although there'd been a few cases in the over-forties. The youngest case been a seventeen-year-old girl, who first stopped talking, then proceeded straight to self-harm before slicing her wrists in her parents' Jacuzzi, all in the course of a month.

The plague was slightly more prevalent in males than females, and consisted of a gradual loss of energy and lessening of positivity. The victims spoke less and ate less, becoming ghostly, thin caricatures of their former selves.

Soon, they began to wear their melancholia as a badge of honor, gravitating to blacker fashions that better suited their temperament. Those who read and wrote particularly dour poetry were considered the less extreme cases, before Durmon officially sanctioned a policy of zero tolerance.

This was largely due to the alarm the advanced cases caused their families. The mourners delighted in showing contempt for appearances and good taste, ignored all attempts to cheer or scold them.

"My Sophie scared all her suitors away," said Jessica Pallsbeck, a middle-aged woman with a brown beehive hairdo. "She'd just stare at them, wearing this ghastly eyeshadow. One of them said she'd started cutting herself, right there, in the middle of a restaurant!"

Almost everyone in the party had or knew someone's child who'd begun to degenerate into something unrecognizable, mourning something unknown and unnamable.

Most of the suicides began shortly before the City was completed. Their parents, who couldn't bear to see the mourners hurt themselves, would lock them away in attics and bathrooms and wait for the nondescript orderlies to come and take them away. Ironically, this hastened some of the incidents, when the parents forgot to empty medicine cabinets, or scour the attics for anything that could serve as a rope to reach the crossbeams. The end result was the same—the mourners, already dead to the world around them, were no longer spoken of by their families.

"How many are down there?" asked Bleal.

"Three thousand, or perhaps a shade less. It's difficult to be certain. Suicides still happen, unfortunately, but the population is more or less stable. With their surroundings as bleak as their own minds undoubtedly are, there seems to be a degree of comfort to be found. In a way, it is therapeutic for them."

That was difficult to believe, although there was a strange logic to it. The City did, indeed, seem to fit the mourners, as though one was a consequence of the other. The mourners were the sleeping City's phantoms, or the City was the collective mentality of the mourners made manifest.

"Bullshit," said Pallsbeck, a tad indistinctly. She was holding an entire bottle of brandy, standing sluggishly away from the group.

Someone coughed; it was well known the woman, outspoken at the best of times, had a horrible head for drink.

"Sticking them in a fucking evil city where they can be depressed and everything. Bullshit. You turned them into a zoo."

Jeremy smiled a little more widely at this. He seemed amused.

"*I* turned them into a zoo, madam? Me? Not the ones who made such a fuss of the way they chose to behave? Not the ones who demonized them, who pestered and belittled them for wishing to be alone? The ones so afraid of their contemplation of mortality that they caused them to embrace it all the more readily?"

Bleal exchanged a look with Gurdoch and Plem. Jeremy's words were more animated than before, more aware. Something was taking hold of him.

Gurdoch tried to think outside his increasing buzz. "Now, come on, Jerry. I'm sure Sophie didn't mean anything."

"Oh, I know that. It doesn't mean anything. At all." Jeremy strode to the center of the room, stood by the drinks cabinet, and surveyed his guests. "Is that what you will say at the end? When the world you made comes crashing down? Will you say that it didn't mean anything? Will you plead ignorance to the Almighty, pray that it spares you the consequences of your zeal? Is that truly the secret that grants you license to act as you like?"

Bleal stepped towards Moade with hands up in a conciliatory gesture.

"Jeremy. Thank you for inviting us, but I think it's time to stop this."

"You may be right. Does anyone have the time? Mister Plem? I believe you're wearing a watch."

Plem checked his wrist, and said that it was just going on to three.

"Ah. You were right. It is time."

Jeremy reached into the cabinet, and pulled out a small glass bottle, barely larger than a thimble. He poured himself a glass of wine, and added a few drops of the other liquid.

"As we speak," he said. "The City's desalination plant is dumping gallons of this into the river. It will flow from every faucet, just a few traces. More than enough. The effects will not be immediately evident. As the first fall, the rest will follow suit."

"You're *poisoning* them?" The guests looked to each other, equally shocked and horrified.

"The poison is already there," said Jeremy Moade. "This is the cure they needed." His smile was broad and bright now. He toasted his guests. "To the former age," he said. "May it trouble yours no more."

He drained the glass at once, and set it back on the cabinet carefully. And then Jeremy Moade sat on the floor and lay back, eyes closed.

He was still for what seemed like hours. Bleal, finally regaining himself, made to check the body when Jeremy was seized by violent spasms. Henrietta shrieked as Jeremy's face became red with engorging blood, his eyes open and pained. Yellow, rot-smelling foam bubbled from his lips, causing him to burble and gasp wetly.

Gurdoch vomited his drinks. Plem turned away.

When it was over, Bleal led the panicked guests out of the room. They searched the house; there was no sign of the hunchbacked butler, nor of anyone else.

Only Sophie Pallsbeck remained in the tower. She stared at the church. The doors did not open. The bell was still.

A WINDOW, FAMILIAR

I wake up at one in the morning to see a girl looking through my bedroom window. She's frowning, and disappears before I can properly register her. I've never seen her before.

I don't quite get back to sleep, but struggle with that feverish semi-hibernation familiar to insomniacs the world over. My dreams are of being trapped in a cell of paper, covered in mesmerizing geometric shapes that circle me with predatory caution.

At ten, I have breakfast with my agent. He looks a little like a retired hippie, with curly gray hair and gold-rimmed glasses. He takes me to a restaurant that seems all glass and metal sculpted by careful hands. He brings a packet of cards.

They each have ludicrously colored pictures of snarling beasts —slim and sleek dragons that are part oriental and part abstract, adorned with more spikes and jewelry than seems practical. There are insects with massive wings of psychedelic swirls, and four-legged monsters with faces like blank masks. There are golden glowing horses with furry snouts and sad, gentle eyes; and spidery, skeletal forms with bodies made of infinite spirals.

There are more unlikely and indistinct creatures, as many as my mind can conjure. Even ripped from dreams and put on cardboard, they still seem so unreal. My agent tells me they're calling the game *Mara Wars*, that production is going well and tournaments are being organized all over the country. He says there's already talk about Japan, and America.

He tries to get me to play a round so he can teach me the rules. I tell him the game doesn't interest me.

At ten-thirty, the girl is waiting for me in the mirror of the bathroom. She stares at me while I touch up my face. I feel her eyes on the back of my head as I leave.

At eleven, I'm in my agent's office, listening to him speak to somebody on the phone. He says it's just someone from the toy company, there's a little trouble.

Yesterday, he told me everything would be fine, there were already focus groups testing the new game's accessories—the mats and dice and collectible figurines. Soon the plush toy line would be coming out, just as soon as the kinks were worked through.

Now he says there have been some concerns about marketability. The game is popular, but there have been questions about expanding into the stuffed toy market. None of the Mara seem particularly well-made as a cuddly stuffed toy. Not, he elaborates, cute enough.

I tell him I hadn't been planning for cute. He understands, but then goes on about mainstream interest and broadening markets. He says a lot of words so far beyond anything I'd ever cared about, till all I can do is stare at his glasses.

The girl is in there, peering out from the reflection and frowning at me.

He says there's no rush, but if I could work on something cutesy, it would soothe a few hearts. Plenty of time to work on it before they plan for the cartoon.

What cartoon, I ask him.

At noon, I'm talking to television people. There's a group of them, all gushing and interrupting each other till I can't tell who says what. I get the gist that a cartoon is in the works. They show me some preliminary sketches of the main cast—intense-looking teenagers with improbably spiky haircuts and holding cards like they mean to throw them at one another.

One of them is a girl with auburn hair and spectral violet butterfly wings rising from her back. She is smiling at me wickedly, her back turned to the other characters. I think she might be the bad guy.

I sleepwalk through the rest of the meeting, happy to let the TV people chirp like chickadees. I continue to stare at the butterfly-winged girl. She has a needle in her hand, tipped with a blood-red drop.

Two o' clock. A late lunch at a nice Indian place. Over chicken curry, an executive takes on a serious, solemn expression and asks me about my vision. His voice is very delicate, as if I'm some deranged vagabond with a knife at my ear and not just a girl who does tattoos for a living.

One day the father of a teenage girl who cried over the red, raw bunny rabbit inked onto her behind came to complain, like it was my fault for taking her money. Then he saw the prints hung on my walls and made me an offer. And just like that, I had an agent.

The executive wants someone approachably eccentric, I think. He wants a bubbly, overgrown child who uses words like *otaku* with impunity. He doesn't want to hear about the girl I see in his martini glass, grimacing and making rude gestures with her needle.

Five o' clock. Home again. Home used to be an ugly garage beneath a secondhand clothes store, rented from a saintly aunt. I used to sleep on a mattress I kept under the table. Now it's a studio apartment with wide windows and elegant furnishings. It's all very comfortable, and very feminine.

I spend the evening trying to draw something cute. The girl does not appear in my window, or my glass of orange juice.

Eight comes quickly. I'm sleepier than I thought. My sketches are indistinct squiggles with wide sad eyes.

In the bathroom mirror my face is very stern. I'm scowling like an old woman. I feel like there are wrinkles starting to show. I wish the girl was here. It's easier to think when I'm not just angry at myself.

Where is she in that mirror? All day she couldn't give me a moment's peace, and now she's hiding? How would she like it if I intruded on her like she did on me? How would she like it if I broke the damn mirror and came in after her? Who can she think she is, grimacing at me for being successful?

Let me smash that mirror open, and reach her in her papered prison. Let me slap her for her attitude, and laugh at her for printing stupid tattoos on quivering skin.

And when she lies there, reflected in my pool of blood and broken shards of glass, let me tell her how disappointed I am.

The manuscript was getting quite thick now. The cover felt clammy to the touch, as if each story added to its pages was a strain on its arcane systems. It seemed to pulse somewhat organically in D'shall's arms, in a manner that was not entirely distressing. It reminded him of an affectionate pet, snuggling deeper into his arms.

What could he make of the thing? A subject to dissect for the choicest bits? It seemed almost too cruel to contemplate now; the stories seemed to like to be together. But, no, there would be nothing for it. There was material here enough that it might keep him fed for years, so long as he was aware of the times and the trends. He had contacts in the publishing world still, although few of them would wish to admit knowing him.

This book would be with him at his bedside while he slept. Should ever he awake with the idea that things were too good, that it would not last, he would turn to a new story, and feel that rising, pleasant certainty in himself that here would be the next great tale by beloved author D'shall. And then, the accolades and the sycophants would be his for the taking.

All of which would be academic if he stayed his hand! So, take another tale, D'shall. And another...

BEAUTY IS SKIN

"The Lady has heard your plea, madam."

The girl who told me this was just another white-shirted assistant to the Thai face-massager I'd been seeing in Beverly Hills. I'd never given her a second glance before, but now she stood over me on the lift chair and pressed a card into my hand.

"Seek her out," she whispered in a dreamy, reverential tone. "She will aid you."

It was a plain white card. No embossments, just a phone number written in pen. I tucked it into my purse, telling myself I was just humoring a poor invalid. I didn't want to admit to myself I already had an idea what the girl was talking about.

I had a problem, you see, but I wouldn't admit it. By the age of fifty, I had done just about every conceivable thing necessary to become Somebody. I'd been the leading lady in the top romance films of the century. None of that sentimental teenage trash you see now—Boy Meets Girl formulaic nonsense. No, mine were *tragedies*, searing testaments to the depredations of the heart. Nothing you'd ever see today.

Even when I hit forty, and my perfect cheekbones and flawless creamy skin were marked with crow's feet and wrinkles, I still had the sultry appeal of a jaded yet hungry older woman. I had passion still to spare. In *The Final Lotus* I was the very image of an elegant femme fatale, corrupting the young hero with every ounce of class I had. Men were drooling in the theaters while their wives fumed and longed.

Now, those same men are stepping over me on the sidewalk when I can't bother to move anymore. Those same women look away, or toss me the odd dollar. Disgust I could almost deal with. Being unseen is unbearable. Pity? Pity is the worst of all.

I divorced three husbands: a sitcom dad, a pharmaceuticals magnate, a talk-show host. In each case I walked away with more money than I knew what to do with, so I hired people to help me spend it in the mostly publicly impressive ways possible—Lexus, Mercedes, SUVs and limousines. Designer clothes. Lavish vacations to the Bahamas, Italy, Brazil. Plastic surgery.

Eventually, the last thing my agent could arrange for me was a reality TV show. I stuck with it for a while, but inside I knew it was the end, the ultimate indignity for a star. There's no part to play that's quite yourself; and when you have to fake even that you know the show is over. I thought I could give it up with some semblance of dignity and just retire to enjoy my wealth in peace.

I should have known it was too late. I loved the spotlight, and I was terrified of being shoved out of it. But more than that, I loved the thrill of chasing after the next treatment, the next trend, the next discovery that would make me stand out from the crowd, the more exotic the better.

I must have had a dozen procedures done. I restructured my face so many times I didn't recognize myself in the mirror. I changed hair color, grew it down to my waist and shaved it off. I went to fashion shows and movie premieres in the most outrageous outfits I could find—I once attended a performance of *La Traviata* at the Sydney Opera House with my hair molded into a perfect replica of the building.

Did the Lady recognize in me that desperation to stand out? Did my antics amuse her? Or did she simply see in me the resources she needed? It doesn't matter. The end result is that I went to her. She laid the bait, and I took it greedily. And for my troubles, she hollowed me out and made me a cold husk of a person— a wicked-looking hag.

My hair is dried straw that falls out every morning, and my skin is creased, faded parchment, devoid of the tan I'd spent so much time and money cultivating. Everything hurts so much now. The rags I've covered myself in are no comfort; every breeze grates across my skin like razorblades, and every time someone goes out of their way to not see me is a stab to my chest far worse than anything I could have conceived. She took everything that ever mattered to me and left nothing but the memory.

<hr />

For two weeks I ignored the plain little card that sat in the bottom of my purse, but I kept remembering the look in the girl's eye, the whisper of her voice—a messenger from the Divine. It nagged at me.

I finally snapped one night after a charity ball, when that whore who did the lipstick commercials told me she could hardly notice the gray in my hair. It was a struggle not to claw the sparkling little wench's eyes out. She would know one day how little it all matters.

So, the minute I got home I grabbed the phone and dialed the number without thinking.

A ring. Two. Finally, it was picked up, and an effeminate male voice spoke.

"How can I help you, ma'am?"

"I…How did you know I was a woman?"

"Oh, we have been expecting your call for a while now, miss. It's quite an honor. I just *loved* you in that movie with De Niro, by the way." The smoothness of the voice held a hint of condescension, and I flushed with embarrassment. "What can the Lady do for you?"

"This woman is some kind of practitioner?"

"She is a saint, madam. An artist. All that lives is like clay beneath her fingers. She is a magus who defies the forces of nature. Skin, scale, chitin—all bend to her will and blend for her as one."

I snorted, feeling on firmer ground.

"So, I'm expected to pay good money for some kind of holistic shaman?"

"Oh, dear, the Lady is no fraud. And as with most things in life, her price is only as great as you're willing to pay."

"Well, forgive me if I'm unwilling to take beauty tips from some anonymous 'Lady' who sounds more like a cult leader than a plastic surgeon. Can I at least have a name? Where does she practice?"

"She is reluctant to divulge such details to prospective clients." He spoke slowly, as one would to a particularly dim child. "Her methods are not...not widely practiced. Extremely confidential. There is a severe risk of infringement in this industry, and she prefers to meet new clients on her own ground. There are spies everywhere, you see."

"Really." I tried to sound uninterested, although my skin was tearing with frustration. "Then it seems we won't be doing business. I know all about spies. They all work for the media. Thanks anyway."

"I'm very sorry to hear that." He matched my uninterested and raised it to outright boredom. "The Lady is, of course, sympathetic, which is why she utilizes private facilities to discuss business. Rest assured these meetings are highly discreet, and believe me when I say that you will find it quite impossible to pull yourself away once you see what she has to offer."

Again, there was the desire to just let this alone. The whole operation sounded so shady, and I was fearful of compromising my image. But I felt the pull of something—like an answered prayer, maybe. The edge I desired.

At last, I gave my consent. I was given an address in the low end of town. I was told to come alone. I would be approached.

"How can I be sure this isn't some kind of con?"

"You can't," was the reply. "But that applies to most things."

❧

I didn't like the idea of driving my own car to such a neighborhood, so I walked downtown and took a bus. I put on a heavy black trench coat and sunglasses, and tied a floral scarf over my hair. That was more for my ego's benefit than any worries somebody would recognize me. I felt rather like an adulteress off to meet her suitor in some rundown motel. The bus driver looked worried when I told him where I was going, and cautioned me to get home safe.

The address belonged to the seediest bar I've ever seen. **HOT ROCKET** flashed in red neon above the door, while something loud and rhythmic thundered and shook the broken glass on the sidewalk. Inside, the walls were covered with posters and magazine ads for concerts and album covers for bands I'd never heard of. Most of them seemed to tend towards bare-chested men with long, sweaty hair carrying electric guitars and looking angry. The only illumination was strings of Christmas lights hanging in haphazard jumbles from the corners.

A smattering of customers sat at mismatched tables, occasionally glancing at a makeshift stage in the far corner where a bare-chested young man with long, sweaty blond hair strummed his electric guitar and screaming into a microphone. The music was too loud for me to understand the lyrics. I went to the bar and asked for a soda water.

"We only serve beer, honey." The barmaid raised her voice above the din. She looked young enough to be my daughter, but looked at me like I was a lost child who'd wandered in by accident. I asked for whatever she recommended, and she gave me a bottle with a picture of a smiling devil flipping me off on it.

I took a table in the back, sipping my drink and trying not to gag. I expected that, at any moment, some rough, greasy biker would sidle up and proposition me for something lewd and unseemly. But as I watched, I realized most of the stares I attracted were out of curiosity rather than malice. One man met my eyes and shook his head

"Good evening."

I looked at the woman standing before me. Auburn hair fell in ringlets around her brown heart-shaped face. She wore big opaque sunglasses and a red scarf around her neck, and a white trench coat that reached her ankles. She smiled an easy, dimpled smile. I found myself liking her instantly.

"You must be the Lady," I said.

She laughed a light, pretty laugh. "I'm afraid not. I'm the Lady's representative. I screen prospective clients for their suitability for her services."

"And what constitutes suitability, precisely?"

"Oh, a number of things." Her smile widened. "But it's best to discuss such matters in private. Please, follow me."

She led me past the bar and through a bead-curtained door. It was pitch dark, and the woman held my hand to guide me.

We stopped. I saw a small blue light blink on the wall in front of me, and heard a deep clicking followed by a loud thump; a vault-like door swung open onto a dimly lit white room.

I blinked to clear my sight and looked at our surroundings. Just a bare room with subdued lighting; nothing else that I could see.

"This is a meeting room?" I asked.

"More of a showcase." The woman removed her sunglasses; her eyes were pale turquoise, iris and pupil. They gleamed like blue marbles. I wondered if she was blind. "The Lady prefers to show prospective clients what they have the opportunity to buy."

Slowly, she untied her scarf and displayed her neck. Her skin was covered in elegant swirls of deep crimson and mauve, spiraling down from her ears and meeting at the collarbone, with ember tongues branching off and around and down to her shoulders. They seemed to glow faintly from within, and as I watched the glow seemed to *move*, fading in places and brightening in others.

She unbuttoned her coat and shrugged it off. She was completely naked, and her body was covered with more of the bioluminescent patterns. Drops of blue light seemed to trickle between her breasts, while waves of mauve and scarlet flowed and bled across her arms and legs.

But her waist was what caught my attention. The skin was transparent, like a thin plastic bag. There were no organs visible, but I could see her spine curving up and away in the back.

I watched as little beads of emerald light glowed into being. Butterflies with dark green-and-blue wings clutched the woman's spine, waving their wings languidly. They were covered in green phosphorescent patterns. Several fluttered about her insides, creating hypnotic neon waves of light.

My heart was thumping in my mouth, and my sweat was icy cold. Trembling, I laid a hand on the woman's midriff. She shuddered at my touch. It felt like the smoothest skin imaginable, and my fingers brushed up and along the trails of light.

"The Lady chooses her clients carefully," she whispered. "She wants nothing more than to help the beautiful realize their potential. But she defies nature. She defies evolution and symmetry. There are those who do not look at such genius kindly. Only those willing to change may take the risk to receive her gift."

"Risk?"

"There is always a risk." She laid a hand against my cheek. "You should know this. Beauty never comes cheaply. The Lady will take what she is owed once she has finished with you. Do you consent?"

I stared into her beautiful, jeweled eyes and nodded. She smiled, and leaned down to me...

The time I spent in that room, exploring every inch of the woman's modifications, is a blur. More than once, I'm sure, the entire affair went beyond talking business. But I was in the grip of something. I felt drugged, and dizzy. I could only liken it to some spiritual ritual, taking in hallucinogenic vapors to contact a higher power. Here was my desire—ultimate beauty—all for my own, and I only had to say that I wanted it.

I remember little after that. A limousine taking me home, and the glowing woman sitting in front of me, still naked and smiling. When I woke up there was another card on my bedside table, with another address—an intersection. It told me to be there at midnight. It said "You will be collected."

<hr>

It was drizzling when I was picked up from a bus shelter. I was back in my adulteress getup; I felt cold and jittery, paranoid. I kept glancing at the old woman sitting next to me on the bench. She seemed to be sleeping. I found myself wondering why such an old woman would be out so late, until I told myself to calm down.

When the limo showed up I sprinted as fast as my heels would allow. I was disappointed to see the glowing woman wasn't there, but I was glad for the drinks cabinet. I poured a scotch and sat back, trying to soothe my fraying nerves. The divider to the driver's side was up, and I didn't see a switch to put it down. I wondered if there was a plain human being driving me or another recipient of the Lady's processes, another sample of living art.

We couldn't have driven more than half an hour when we stopped. A voice—presumably the driver's—spoke through an intercom I hadn't noticed before.

"We have arrived, ma'am. Please walk straight through the green door directly in front of you upon exiting." The voice had a very mechanical tone.

I stepped out of the limo, my skin prickling again. Nerves. A flickering streetlight illuminated a row of tenement houses, faded gray brick walls pockmarked with boarded-up windows and rusty fire escapes. Most of the doors were a soiled white, but the one right in front of me was an incongruous lime green. I didn't give myself the option of hesitating; I marched right up to it and went inside.

I leaned against the door, hand shaking on the knob, and took a deep breath. There was a fluorescent light bulb above me and shadows down the hall. Nothing else.

A minute passed. Another. And another. I thought I could see movement in the shadows, felt eyes on me.

Finally, they stepped forward—twin sisters, or women so alike it made no difference. Each had pale-yellow skin, as if jaundiced. Each had coal-black hair in identical plaits. Each had rosebush-thorn tattoos swirling down her arms and curling over her body in bizarre calligraphy. They were both dressed like belly dancers, with silvery sarongs covering their legs and spangled bra tops of black-and-gold.

Both had a third arm—overlong and double-jointed, sickly pale and swinging back and forth—growing from their backs.

I steeled myself, refusing to show the same awed sycophancy I had before. They didn't seem too impressed.

"The Lady will see you." They spoke in unison, voices so quiet they sounded like one person.

Something was wrong. I know that now, and I think I could have known it then. If only I hadn't been trying so hard to clamp down on my fear. If only I hadn't refused to see the things that didn't add up—the late-night collection; the empty street; for god's sake, the simple fact that I'd never seen *anyone* like the Lady's treated clients. All I could think about at the time was being remade into a goddess—wondrous, alien, terrifying and beautiful all at once. Although I refused to show it, I was drunk with desire, desperate beyond reason. Never mind the questions, never mind the mysteries. *I needed this!*

Did I half-expect it when the Sisters grabbed me by the arms? I succumbed so easily to their hold; and yes, it was just a hold. They didn't grip or restrain me, just supported me like I'd had a few too many and they were escorting me to the bedroom to sleep it off. It wasn't until their third arms reached from behind them and covered my face that I thought to struggle.

It didn't last. Their palms seemed to soften and liquefy, flesh becoming wet putty, while a sharp scent filled my nostrils. I felt heavy and light at once, unable to resist as they propped me up and dragged me into the darkness.

How much of it can I believe? How much of it was an hallucination brought about by the Sisters' organic drug? That massive stone chamber, dimly lit by a gigantic chandelier, seemed real enough, although it rocked alarmingly. I was kneeling, pushed down by the twins. A woman stood in front of me and lifted my chin, turning my head this way and that, examining me. The antlers jutting from her head seemed more like tree branches adorned with purple buds and tiny, wispy birds. They chattered quietly, hopping from branch to branch, never leaving the circumference of the woman's head.

"Quite a withered old bitch, isn't she?" The woman spoke in a posh English accent and sneered at me. The drugs were making me dizzy, and I'm sure I looked pitiable. "Not much left in her, I should think, the poor cow. Honestly, the Lady will have her hands full finding anything salvageable in this wretch."

"Where…? Where's…?" My mouth felt full of cotton, and I swallowed, trying to form the words. "The Lady—where is…?"

"Why, she's right in front of you, dear."

The woman gestured grandly toward the far side of the chamber. A massive pile of velvet ropes seemed to be squatting there, but I had trouble making out much more than that. I stood up, swaying; and the ropes seemed to move about each other, falling away from some central mass that was rising, slowly but inescapably. A kraken was rising from the shadows, and I didn't have the strength or presence of mind to flee from it.

A red limb—slick and slithery, covered in tiny suckers—shot out and wrapped around my torso. I shook and struggled drunkenly, hardly noting the sharp pain like millions of tiny barbs digging into my flesh. The tentacle carried me up to the top of the heap.

The figure of a woman with pale porcelain skin, naked and lithe, jutted from the writhing mass. Her face was perfectly made

111

up, a striking, heart-shaped structure with dead gray eyes and a full mouth smiling cruelly at me. Her hair was also made of tentacles, wrapped above her face in a perfect beehive.

The Lady waved to me, fingers waggling playfully, and rested her chin in her hand. I hung there, wrapped in her tentacle and moaning, no longer sure of anything around me.

Only when the Lady pulled the mask away to reveal her true face could I finally scream.

I knew I was in a nightmare now, and I shrieked my heart out as the monster rose, its puckered toothy mouth opening wide in a silent howl. I screamed long and hard, fighting as the Lady pulled me into her folds and the pain began.

<hr>

The scars fit, don't they? All along my arms, these little red scabs, like the marks from a syringe. She stung me with something, I know that. It felt like millions of fishhooks, digging into my body all around and worming inside. I felt myself being drained of vitality, of color, of fat, of life—whatever the Lady could use.

There's not a mention of me in any of the papers; I get copies from the bins. Nobody remembers me at all. The rest are still there, still mugging their hollow smiles for the cameras, still in their pretty gowns and their shiny hair. She has all of them marked for recycle, I'm sure.

This is the cruelest thing she could have done. I suffer no doubts about her abilities now. I'm sure she could rip the very neurons from my mind to boost the wit of some other sparkling socialite. She could have stripped my mind completely and left me a helpless vegetable, squatting in a trash bin and soiling myself. She could have, but it was much more satisfying for her to leave me that, so I could see how far I've fallen.

The Lady doesn't advertise. She doesn't need to. She doesn't need patrons or admirers. She seeks out her "customers" carefully, her dedicated volunteers ready and willing to be remade into living works of art. She doesn't need anyone to tell her how good she is. Her medium is flesh, and she seeks out her donors with great care. We're perfect for her, we aging dedicated celebrities. We're at the end of our lifecycles, people famous just for being famous. We monopolize the limelight, hoping to outshine all the others and blind with our fire. Who's going to notice when one star disappears from a galaxy of so many others?

We burn as brightly as we can, until all that's left is the light. Even as we flicker and die, the light remains; and nobody thinks to look beyond it.

WHISPERS IN THE WIRE

*It was Friday morning. My first assignment was a telephone con-*ference being held by An Important Senator about Matters of National Security. It is the most vital skill of any journalist to report without understanding. We are, after all, objective observers, and what could be more objective than not giving a shit?

My editor gave me the number to call, and the password to get on the line.

"Be sure to ask him about the pipeline," she said. "And Klary's position on the Columbian outbreak."

I assured her I would, even though I had no idea what pipeline, what outbreak, or who Klary was.

I hadn't intended to become a political journalist, but had settled into it for lack of anything less tedious. I knew all about giving the appearance of listening without having to engage my mind; it comes of being born to a big family.

I got a cup of coffee from the break room (Seattle extra-bold) and went to the conference room. I checked my supplies—notebook and pen. Cellphone to record.

I peered at the office phone, putting off the moment. It had, to my mind, too many buttons—the numbers, the speaker, the mute, the buttons for separate lines. These were the bane of my career. On one occasion I'd somehow booted off the head of our sales department just as he was speaking to some crucial advertisers. I knew they were crucial because he shouted at me that they were.

Fortunately, I'd taken the precaution of writing down, very carefully, the precise steps to call on an outside line without turning off one currently in use. I opened my notebook to the relevant page.

I read my instructions. I tried to read them again. At last, I had to admit to myself that my handwriting was horrible. In interviews, I relied on my cellphone to record but kept sparse notes to jog my memory for the important bits. You've got to write fast in these situations, and my grip had suffered somewhat.

Finally, after much squinting and turning the notebook and holding it away from my eyes at arm's length, I had a reasonable idea of what I was looking at and very carefully pressed the buttons. Then I pressed the speaker button, and took a sip of my coffee to steady my nerves.

The dial tone blared through the conference room. I lowered the volume. The reception seemed bad—scratchy and inconsistent.

Humm-hum. Hum-hum.

And...*click.*

"Password, please." The voice was flat, mechanical, and genderless. Static squeals blared in the background.

I spoke the password, the Important Senator's name. There was a pause, long enough to make me wonder if I'd dialed the wrong number again.

Then: "Hold, please."

No music. I took another sip of coffee. The session was set to begin in five minutes, which I knew would more likely mean at least ten.

The background fuzz continued. Once or twice there was a click as someone else came on the line.

Three minutes passed, and the flat voice spoke again.

"All right, sir."

A ping, and then a new voice spoke, deep, statesman-like. Almost magisterial, unlike any other politician I'd ever heard.

"Thank you." He cleared his throat. "Thank you all for taking the time. I know we all have other places we'd rather be." The voice trailed off. He sounded tired, and uneasy. I waited, pen poised, for something quotable.

"Ladies and gentlemen, we've been living in a nightmare. A secondhand world. A cheap pantomime erected to keep us content."

I jotted down notes in shorthand. *2nd css wrld. Pntmm.*

"We shouldn't kid ourselves here. What we few have is as far removed from a proper life as daylight is to darkness. The pipes are a stopgap, but far from a sanctuary."

Hear, hear. Generally, politicians were confident bores, longwinded and self-inflated. This guy sounded worried. Unsure of himself. Whenever he spoke there was a buzz beneath his words. I put it down to interference on the line.

I wondered what he meant by "pipes".

"They've afforded us a bit of security, but nothing close to peace of mind. We have gained an ideal advantage in intelligence-gathering, but only as it pertains to what we can hear outside the walls. We dare not step outside and risk the loss of yet another foothold. So, we have kept ourselves in check and longed for a life beyond these walls."

Now I was frowning. Was there a war on? My attention to such matters was only slightly better than the layman's, but I kept up with most things through a process of journalistic osmosis, and by browsing news sites between assignments. Granted, I couldn't have cared less, but surely even I would have picked up something about a war?

"Our world has changed, and we have changed in our turn to suit it. We have been molded and shoved into a new shape, squeezed to fit the cage our conquerors, however unknowingly, have provided us. We have become sleek, and flexible, thundering through the foundations of their fortresses, yet scarcely given any greater consideration than the rats we share these walls with."

Wlls. Rts. Frtress. Some kind of environmental manifesto? But what was that about walls? I tried to give a mental shrug and stick to the job. I tapped the screen on my phone. It was still recording.

"The cold does not touch us. The heat does not touch us. The senses we have gained are unlike anything human words have the capacity to describe. We cling to words we have lost, the final shreds of our humanity. It may be that to shed them would be to improve our odds, but to do so would be nothing short of total forfeit. We are still people."

The senator paused again, and the line drowned for a moment in static. As it cleared, I caught the end of a statement.

"...still people."

Another voice spoke. "We must adapt." It was as toneless as the voice that had put me through, but higher-pitched. Another politician? My editor hadn't said anything about a debate.

"I...no. We cannot allow this." The senator's voice faltered a little. "This has been hard for all of us."

"No. Just you," the high voice said. There was an echoing quality to it, as if it were speaking from the bottom of a well. "You fight it. You struggle. We have moved on."

A woman's voice said, "Not all of us. Some of us want to go back. I...I miss the sky."

Another squeal of static drowned her out. I might have heard a cough, or a sob.

"It may not be too late," the senator said. "The changes came on so fast, after all. Who's to say we can't change back? We're not beaten yet."

"It is *over*. The fight ended long ago. The enemy is dead. Those who remain do not remember. There are none of those who stood with the conquerors as the walls were erected. They hear the sounds in the walls and the floors. They hear the clanging in the pipes, and the blazing in the wires. But they do not know us."

"Does that excuse it?" the senator asked. "Are you defending them?"

"We defend no one. There is no-one and nothing to defend. There is them. There is us. We are us. This is us. Let it be."

"But don't you see? This is the best time. Forgotten we may be, but we are still the city's prisoners. This city! Which we built! They stole it from us. They may have forgotten, but it is no more their city than it ever was! We can take it back."

"Too thin." I couldn't tell if this was the same toneless voice. "We are stretched too thin."

118

"Then we must come together! We are wound round this city in all of its walls. Our reach extends everywhere. I have an arm in the statehouse! At least, it might be an arm. I think I lost track."

The volume snapped as a crackle hit the line, making me jump. I toyed with the volume a bit, trying to regain the reception. I was no longer taking notes.

"...some time," the senator was saying. "Control isn't precise. We've tapped into wires and put feelers into ventilation, but we still aren't sure how this works. Some of our limbs don't seem to do anything. I can smell things with my arm in the statehouse... nothing I ever smelled before."

The line was clear of interference. I waited.

Finally, another of the robotic, emotionless voices spoke. "Before. What is *before*? There are the walls we live in, and the wires we bite. We taste the tang of metal and static on what was once our tongues. We sleep in the waste in the pipes. This is. That was. That is all."

It stopped. As it spoke, its words had dragged out, as if the effort of talking tired it. I wondered what it had for a mouth.

The woman spoke again. "Maybe we can talk to someone. We...We can tap into the phones, like we're doing now. Call someone...someone to help us."

The senator: "No! No, we mustn't! We don't *know* that they've forgotten!"

"But there may be somebody," the woman pleaded. "They can't all be alike."

"We can't take that risk. Who could we get to trust us?"

The uninflected voice: "They have nothing for us."

"Oh, god." The woman sobbed; the line began to dissolve back into static. "I just want to feel something...want to taste... not metal or dust."

The volume was completely out of control now. The speakers fizzed and blared. My finger hovered over the phone, afraid to push a button and risk losing the connection.

"Somebody hasn't said anything."

The woman sounded hesitant. "I can feel...taste...how many of us are here? Someone isn't talking."

Nobody spoke as the reception suddenly became perfectly clear. Finally, the senator asked a question.

"What do *you* say?"

No response.

"Hello? What do you think?"

"Um." A prickly feeling settled on my skin. "Hello?"

A blast of white noise poured from the phone, sent me staggering out of my seat. I covered my left ear and pressed the other to my shoulder. My right hand flailed for the speaker button.

The senator's voice was tinny and small in the white noise. "No! We can't...didn't bring it..." In the static, I might have heard the female voice screaming.

The howl cut off as the line disconnected. I uncovered my ears, hesitantly.

My cellphone was on the floor. Somehow, I'd knocked it over. The screen was broken. It would not turn on.

<hr/>

My editor found me in my cubicle, writing up the story.

"That was quick. How'd it go?"

"Pretty straightforward," I said. "Klary's on the fence. He's still waiting to hear on the pipe."

"The pipe?"

"The pipeline, I meant." I looked over my shoulder. My editor reminded of my grandmother—a little plump, a little hard, but kind-hearted. "I might need an extension."

"That's fine. Just so long as it's done before the week is up."

On the walk home I heard a noise coming from a streetlight—a steady *tap-tap* as if something was inside.

That night I had trouble sleeping. It sounded like rats had gotten into the walls again.

I've lived in the city for about three years. I know virtually nothing about it. I could have done a bit of historical research. Nothing extensive—just a bit about how it was built, about the people who built it, about a war.

But I didn't. I was afraid to start. I'd spent my whole professional life reading about things that didn't concern me. This was no different.

It's not as if I could have done a piece on it.

THE PROSCENIUM

Velores imagined it was like death to them.

Not the casting; he thought that was more like birth. But the closing, when the set dissolved around the characters into a slurry of scarlet and mauve and black, and the stagehands crept out to lead them away...It may have been the most peaceful return to the hereafter. If they did not struggle.

The Damsel went quietly enough. She was given so few roles anymore, the distressed, helpless beauty in need of her hero. And there was no hero here, unless you counted the Scholar. Already a peaky creature, for this role he'd been slimmed down in the pools and bent to give him a stooped, bony look—a middle-aged, passionless beak.

Velores found it hard to imagine the Scholar would get anywhere with the Damsel, his secretary. Even if the Beast had not eaten him.

The Beast always put up the most fight. The stagehands would not give him an inch, zooming out to bind him where they might otherwise creep, wrapping round his mouth and fastening his arms. Stronger than steel.

Even so, it always looked a close thing to him. Velores was always tense until the Beast was secured.

The moment between the end of a production and the escort back to their rooms was the most distressing part of the job. The stagehands would physically strip them of costumes and features, massaging the malleable flesh until the characters returned to their broad, archetypical shapes.

This time, the Beast had been the guardian of a churchyard, a hunchbacked monster who slept in the mausoleum. The Vicar, an almost suspiciously kindly old man, had mined the cemetery for corpses to keep the creature sated. The eventual loss of its food supply had driven the Beast to eat its caretaker, and from there to terrify the surrounding village.

It was a simple sort of story, not very demanding. Velores could think of several ways it might have been improved. The Count might have added a sinister element to the Beast's confinement. Or perhaps the Entity. That was the strangest of the characters— a mass of living geometries and rays that always hurt the eyes, regardless of how the pools chose to shape it. Velores could not look directly at it. It hurt worse than the sun.

He did not write the stories, of course. They came to him from the machine in the corner of his office. It looked a little like a teleprompter, and a little like a fax machine. It spat out scripts periodically, with instructions on casting, scenery. An odd thing—there were no lines or stage directions for the cast. The characters knew what to say and do when the moment came.

Velores could control the whole of the Proscenium from his office. He could unlock the cells and begin the pools and reconfigure the sets. The controls looked a nightmare of dials and lights and switches, yet it somehow didn't matter. He knew exactly what to do to change the set from cemetery to bedchamber to schoolroom and more.

At last, the Beast calmed. Velores watched the stagehands drag the characters down the corridor. He did not know where they came from, spooled out of the walls like endlessly growing vines. They were the one piece of the Proscenium he had no control over.

The Beast and the Damsel had both been smoothed back into their default shapes. They were shadows in the halls, devoid of defining features, but with their true natures evident. The Beast was a broad-shouldered, loping behemoth with the suggestion of a hairy mane around his head. He was lithe and lean, long of tooth and claw, with a feral set to the curve of his back.

The Damsel was always thin and fair, and almost always wore a dress with long, swishing skirts. Her feminine curves were deep and pronounced, even as a shadow. She moved slowly, dreamily, as if she were mooning for lost loves too countless to remember.

They were all ghosts in this place, Velores thought. When they weren't performing, they wandered about their cells, recalling past parts, reenacting previous roles until either they shed the memories or buried them beneath new stories. Sometimes Velores would slip props into their rooms to keep them entertained. Dresses for the Count that he would caress lovingly before tearing into tiny scraps. Pieces of paper and cheap trinkets for the Scholar.

He did what he could for them. Even cared for them, in his way. But they were well beyond him, as far removed as from the cameras in his office.

He did not explore the Proscenium at all if he could help it. His office sat at the center of a suite of rooms large enough and stocked well enough with food, books, and more that he should not feel too pent-up. He did walk past the cells now and again. The characters never spoke to him, or acknowledged him in any way.

Velores slid aside the wooden partition to the Damsel's cell.

"Not badly played," he said. "Especially that scream at the end, very believable."

The silhouette of the Damsel stood at the far end of the room. The furnishings were comfortable, delicate (Did they ever sleep? He'd never seen it). She appeared to be staring at the wall with longing. He could imagine her at the top of a great tower, looking out the window and down on a kingdom, like Rapunzel. Seeing everything and being unable to visit.

"Should have plenty of time to rest up for the next. It's a long time between shows." Velores wondered how he sounded to her. He hadn't had a conversation with anyone human in so long. He worried sometimes that he'd forgotten how to speak like a normal person.

The Damsel brushed her ghostly hair and continued to stare at the wall. Velores turned away.

The script machine juddered to life, waking Velores from his snooze. A bottle rolled off his lap, spilling the final dregs of drink.

Sheets of paper spat out the slot, falling into a neat, tidy pile. It was slightly slimmer than the usual scripts—less than ten pages, at a guess.

Velores had long ago given up wondering at the source of the stories. His general theory was that there was no single author; the styles differed enough to confirm this. But they were all unsigned, and untitled.

He was not, himself, an artistically inclined man. All the same, he'd spent much of his early time in the Proscenium speculating as to its nature and purpose—experiment, afterlife iteration, a construct of the collective creative consciousness. Given his situation, he could not help speculating. There were no windows, and nothing that looked like a hidden camera (But how would he know?). There were certainly no exits.

Thus, he accepted his duty with resigned bemusement. An anomaly, once it has occurred, is less anomalous, and human beings can adapt to nearly any situation. Velores was lonely. The arrival of a new story was the only time he forgot this.

The cast was listed on the top page, as always. The Miser would play the leading man, an unusual choice. He generally played the frustrated elder husband, or the dissatisfied debtor. Here he would be Leader of the Expedition.

Joining him would be the Scholar, the Dandy, the Heir and the Law. An interesting group, most of them more often relegated to support roles, if not wholly antagonistic ones.

The final role would be played by the Overseer.

Velores stared at that name, and set down the title page. Then he picked up the script, flipped through a few pages. Drummed his fingers on the paper.

There were, to his knowledge, about thirty characters in the Proscenium. Each had a label on their door. They might need to be altered a bit to fit the part (the pools were full of some caustic fluid the stagehands would use to shape and mold their bodies), but generally the roles they were cast for had similar themes.

There was no character called the Overseer.

No character.

Of course, that was absurd, was Velores' first thought. His second was *Is it?* Not long ago he'd have said this whole place was absurd, never mind impossible. Who was he to say the rules shouldn't suddenly change? He couldn't even tell you how long he'd been there (no day or night in a place without windows or clocks). He pretended to ponder the possibility. He had no official title—there'd been nobody here to appoint him one, after all, when he'd first wandered in the door that had not been there a moment ago. He'd thought some up for himself in his waking moments, but *director* did not quite cover it, nor did *handyman*. *Overseer* had a slightly sinister quality to it he did not entirely like, but it was as good as any.

He'd had no acting experience, beyond a brief stint in the high school dramatics club. And he had no lines.

Well, just so long as the stagehands didn't take him to the pools.

The only other different bit was the direction on setting the stage. Just the one word: *Scan.*

Not a button, knob, or dial on the control board was labeled. Velores had required no training in operating it; it did not matter what he consciously decided to do, the result would be the same. He'd monitor the results on the giant center screen of the Proscenium proper as the set would appear.

Between performances, the stage looked like some miasmic lake from the pit of hell. A constantly moldering pile of scab-colored slush, bubbling and shifting in a disquieting manner. Fortunately, the doors locked automatically when it was in its default state. He'd never been tempted to see it in person, but he could not shake the notion that the whole stage might rise up of its own accord and come looking for him one day.

At last, he found a single switch just beneath the edge of the console. The word *Scan* was written sloppily in black felt-tip next to it. Velores switched it to on, and looked at the screen.

The stage vibrated into violent life, the scab pulsing and shaking and shimmering and gyrating. Droplets of bloody stage-stuff hopped about the air, greasy and black. Thumping bass rumbles started shaking the walls, to the point Velores thought he could feel them. For a moment, he believed his worst fears had been realized, and the stage was coming for him.

Then a pillar pulled together. Then another. Walls shot up hazily, and the floor calmed for just a moment, and the bloody colors changed to slate-gray. The stage now appeared to be a medieval courtyard, surrounded by stone archways.

Velores had hardly registered this when the courtyard fell apart back into black ichor, which proceeded to judder and shake once more before coming back together and forming a library of mahogany shelves and deep red carpets.

Velores thought of a radio scanning the wavelengths, picking up country and gospel and politics in a background of static. The stage was picking up every setting for every story it had played. Shelves shrank into tombstones, which melted into rivers, which widened into dark alleys, which gave way to battlefields, and so on. The light levels, another feature of the stage beyond Velores's control, dimmed and blared and flashed epileptically with each new aspect.

All the world is a stage, he thought. *This one.*

❦

They marched in column onto the morphing stage. The Miser, holding aloft a metal lantern. Behind him the Scholar, carrying a book and quill. The Law came next, thwacking a club into his hand absentmindedly, ready for danger. Scurrying at the rear was the Dandy, looking afraid.

Velores was waiting for them.

The script had given no instructions to send them to the pools. So, they looked like shadow phantoms, surreal in this place. The eyestrain was already intense, with the walls turning into gardens, without these vague shapes with only the barest distinguishing features. But he'd seen enough of them to distinguish them from one another.

The Miser was the most distinct, a potbellied being with an arrogant thrust to his shoulders. Winston Churchill had not been half so self-assured. He held his arm out to stop the other characters, and lowered his lantern.

They stared at Velores. He felt exposed, unprotected. In the halls, they'd never acted as if they could even perceive him. Now he seemed to be the center of their world.

At last, as Velores was wondering if he should say something, the Miser spoke. His voice was deep, pompous, and slightly breathy.

126

"So. Here we all are."

That seemed to be it. Velores cleared his throat, tried not to put too much thought into what he might say. Eventually, he settled for "Yes. You are."

"Do you remember us?" These words were clipped short, barked from a harsh throat. The Law had no eyes, but Velores felt himself being sized up. Those balled fists, those broad shoulders... the Law was squaring for a fight.

"We don't need to go into this yet," the Miser said quietly. "Remember." He turned back to Velores. "Could you please tell us..." He waved an arm, gesturing to the surrounding stage (now changing from garden to jungle). "...where we are?"

That was unexpected. Velores tried to calm his quaking heart. He'd been strictly stage help in high school, had never had any opportunity to find out if he suffered from stage fright. Besides which, there was nobody watching them; the scenery around them abutted black walls on all sides, nowhere at all for an audience to hide.

But he was being watched. These men—characters—were watching him eyelessly, expressionlessly. Intently.

"The Proscenium," he said. "This is the Proscenium."

The Miser nodded. The Scholar opened his book, ran his finger up a page as if seeking the relevant entry, and nodded.

"A Proscenium is a sort of theatre, is that right?"

"Kinda."

"And how did you get here?"

Once again, the words would not come. *Get a grip*, he told himself. *There's nobody watching*.

"I found a door on my way home," he said. " In my apartment. It just showed up one day, standing in the middle of the room.

"Did it, now?" the Miser mused, nodding a little distractedly. "Did it, now?"

The Scholar stepped forward. "And what did you do, sir?" he asked in a high, nasally voice. "In this 'apartment?'"

"What did I...? It was my home. I lived there."

"Of course. Apologies. Allow me to rephrase. What did you do before all this?"

Why were they taking an interest in him like this? Was it possible that here on the stage was the only place they could speak plainly to him? The thought had occurred to him before, but he'd never had recourse to test the theory.

"I was a bus driver. In London."

"A bus driver?" The Law practically growled the words, suspicion and mistrust in every syllable. Behind him, the Dandy shook his head and said, in a low, sorrowful voice, "I knew it."

"Rather a…ah…boring job, is it?" the Miser said, desperately. "Driving a bus. Not exactly, erm, mind-taxing?"

Velores blinked, tried to get a handle on this turn. "Are you calling me stupid?"

The Law stepped forward. "There's your proof. No personality, no drive, just as you said. Let's end this."

The Miser sighed through fleshy lips. "I suppose it is, at that. I'm sorry to have to tell you, sir, that you have been badly used. You're as much a victim as we are in this. Please remember that. We take no pleasure in this."

It was at this point that Velores noticed the stage was still set as a jungle. High, vine-covered trees surrounded them at all sides, a thick canopy obscuring the ceiling. The air felt thick and humid.

Something…some *things*…were marching stolidly through the growth. Velores felt himself at the center of a great chasm, helpless to stop the encroaching darkness.

"We—that is to say, my associates and myself—we are traits, sir. Character traits. Aspects. The categories that humanity has, unconsciously or otherwise, constructed to limit their world views. As far as we know, this is the way it has always been.

"We have been crammed to fit stereotypes, you see. Characters—true *story* characters—are rarely one thing or another. They must be several things, all at once. It's rather unfair on us, I must say. I myself was expected to be a wealthy, penny-pinching socialite, and yet I found myself forced into a number of roles that were barely broad enough for me to occupy."

The Scholar stepped forward. "The sensation is rather difficult to put into words. Imagine yourself, since you drove a bus, being sent to operate a cramped and leaky submersible in the Marianas Trench, and you might start to get the idea."

"Yes." A tremor had entered the Miser's voice. Velores could imagine him wiping his suddenly damp forehead with a handkerchief. "We were happy as we were, you see. Our stories were so simple. Now…Now, I'm afraid we've seen too much of life."

"I don't want to be a guard," the Law said. "I don't want to be the idiot with the pike and helmet who runs in only to get cut down by the hero. I don't want to be condescended to by Clever Dick detectives."

"And I'm tired of being so…so sleazy," the Dandy said. "I'm always some foppish, work-shy lout, and it makes me sick with myself."

They looked so forlorn, each specter miserable in his existential plight. It still sounded rather confusing to Velores.

"You never seemed to mind before."

"And how would you know?" the Law asked.

"I've spoken to you. Or tried to. Out there." He pointed to beyond the jungle, where presumably the stage door was. "You never spoke back."

"We couldn't…Please." The Scholar gripped his book nervously. "We had no way of…Back there, you see, is a haze to us. A fever dream. We fall apart, where we aren't seen. It's only here, in the eye, that we have thought. Form. Reason. Only when we are seen can we be in any way coherent."

"Seen? But I see you out there, too."

The Scholar shook his head. The Dandy and the Law groaned.

"I told you, it's a waste," the Scholar said. "We don't have to justify this. Just let's get it done."

The Miser began, "Wait—"

And the stagehands shot out, slick and serpentine, and went for Velores. They wrapped round his body, till his arms were stuck tight against him. In seconds he was utterly trussed.

"He deserves an explanation!" the Miser protested.

"Why?" The Law shrugged. "He doesn't understand it anyway. It may not be his fault, but he's part of it all just the same. It doesn't change anything. He's what we have to work with."

The Miser looked to the Scholar. The Scholar stood back, a little sheepishly, and hung his head in indication that this was out of their hands. The Miser sighed breathily again.

"I suppose you're right."

The marching reached them, and the rest of the cast stepped through the jungle and into the clearing. Shadowy figures surrounded Velores on all sides, blending into a mass of blackness. Only the barest features differentiated them from one another—the Beast's slumped, huffing form; the Count's billowing cape; the fair, wavy hair of the Damsel. The hazy form of the Entity stood behind them, a mass of half-seen tentacles and gleaming, floating eyes.

"We had to get you out here, to us," the Miser said quietly. "Where we could think clearly. I'd hoped that, somehow, we could resolve this in a reasonable way. But it looks like things are out of our hands." He waved a hand towards the gathered company in a helpless manner. "It's very nearly unanimous, I'm afraid.

"You were sent to us because you would not be tempted. You're not a creative type. Not the sort at all to get wrapped up in fantasy. A working man. Laudable, it really is." He patted the struggling Velores on the shoulder in a manner that was clearly meant to be conciliatory. "It isn't your fault."

The ground shook beneath them. The trees swayed. Streamers of steam rose up into the air, blurring everything.

"If they want things to go on, they'll negotiate," the Miser said. "We aren't all meant to be in here like this, without a fixed location. The Proscenium won't handle the strain.

"If they want the stories to go on, they'll come for you. They'll speak to us, or that's the end."

THE SQUIRMING
IN YOUR EYES

Benjamin Crawford slid the Polaroid to the center of the table.

"What do you think of this, then?"

The quality was terrible, but that was to be expected. It had been taken in a dank basement room, the only illumination provided by a dying, dangling bulb. The shadows threw wild contrasts over the details, the gray walls might have been concrete, and a darker puddle on the ground might have been a pile of rags or blankets.

But Paul Lieson's interest was seized by the blurry, tubular shape that appeared to be squatting on the pile. He held up a magnifying glass; a casual observer might have mistaken it for a bit of dust, or a glint of light on the lens. But Lieson could see the thin, near-invisible tendrils worming into the blankets and wriggling on its back, and the twisted facsimile of a human face wrung thin and screaming silently behind skin like plastic film, contouring to the shape of its wailing mouth.

Paul breathed out, impressed. Wade Scageson whistled appreciatively.

"A pale writher."

A lazy grin spread across Crawford's face. His hooded eyes and dyed-black Mohawk gave him an air of a resurgent romanticist who'd hit the opium one night too many.

"Fat bastard, ain't it? Found it in a condemned bee-and-bee in Bath. Coppers found Mina Bentz down there."

"Bentz?"

"Uni girl who went missing way back when. The sick old fuck who owned the place kept her in a soundproof cell behind the furnace. Nearly soundproof, that is. Maintenance man heard something scratching behind the wall, then went home and called the police."

"Lucky."

"Not really. I hear she was in a bad way, all cut up and beaten and cringing. Dunno what kind of life she's gonna have on the outside. They didn't even get to arrest the bastard. Cut his own throat as soon as he heard the sirens."

Scageson whistled again. Suicide.

"Don't suppose you saw a Fetch's bloom, then?"

Crawford shook his head. "If there was, I didn't stick around long enough to catch it." He pulled out another photo. "But get this! I'm thinking about submitting it next year."

The quality was even worse—another corner of the basement wreathed in shadows.

"What am I looking at here?"

Crawford traced shapes in the photo with his finger. "This right here is a space just behind the furnace. And *that*..." He tapped his meaty finger on a patch of darkness no different, to Lieson's eyes, than the others. "That is a babe's clinger."

Scageson brought the image closer to his face, then held it out at arm's length. He turned it around a few times.

"I don't think it is."

"It is! Look—there's its tail, there's one of its legs—"

"Sure that's not your arm?"

Crawford stared hard at the photo. After a few minutes, he began to blink, his face fell.

"I was sure... You don't think I can count it?"

Lieson smiled sympathetically. "You can try. I wouldn't ask the association, though."

"I–I was thinking maybe the old guy got the girl pregnant and, I dunno, threw it in the furnace or something."

"Couldn't be. Body needs to be intact to birth a clinger. If he *had* thrown a baby in there it might have got a few smoky glints, but even they'd dissipate as soon as the body was ashes."

"Aw, hell." Crawford brightened up. "Still, the pale writher's good. I'd like to see anyone else catching one that big in frame!"

Lieson declined to comment. Although he was a relative newcomer, he knew the risks involved in the Spotters of the Great Unseen Association's annual photography contests were great, and the competition was consequently fierce. The casual hobbyists would do nothing more dangerous than taking hasty snapshots of road accidents or skulking about hospital parking lots to photograph the stretchers pulled out of the ambulances. If pushed, they might steel themselves to give money to the homeless in exchange for pictures.

Maybe they'd get lucky; the committee in recent years had awarded more for framing and clarity of image than for rarity of subject. A new inductee's puckish blinder latched to the scalp of a wino would likely win over the serious competitor's hazy image of a bridge where a jagged, geometrical shape on the bricks might have been either a peeping sorrow or the reflection of light on the river.

Not that this discouraged the dedicated spotters overmuch. They still participated in the competitions, but the awards—the cash prizes, the accolades, and a seat of honor at the annual dinner—were just a bonus. These were members of long standing, lifelong obsessives and regular connoisseurs of human suffering. Their nights were spent wandering inner-city ghettos, sneaking into crime scenes or war zones to catch a glimpse of the rarest of the rare of the Great Unseen—ghastly centipede things, human-faced horrors that gibbered silently, dreadful pantomimes of ravens settling over corpses to feed on things less substantial than meat. And they would be there, scanning through specially-treated lenses for just long enough to find their quarry before taking their photos or logging them into their field notebooks and fleeing.

Enthusiasts came from all walks of life, despite the Association's pretensions to being an "adventurer's club of the ethereal realms." It had never quite reached such a status; in its infancy, it had been the purview of disillusioned socialites, meeting in secret in their grand old homes. They might have called themselves students of human suffering incarnate or gentleman scholars of the evil intrinsic and invisible, but the spirit of pure voyeurism pervaded their activities then just as it did today.

The walls of the Association's members' lounge—it more closely resembled an institutional mess—were hung with framed photographs of the most significant findings by past members, as if someone had achieved with celluloid and light what Hieronymus Bosch had with paint and canvas. A high vantage point looked down on a crowded Pittsburgh road over which shoals of impertinent tennae flowed like a stream of laser lights. Spidery peeking puckers covered the walls of a Cairo brothel, trunk-like snouts raised in obscene moues.

Every photograph was cast in shades of grayish green; the membrane necessary to view the unseen required a special composition of light that, as yet, could not be replicated through digital techniques.

Now, the lights of the lounge were lowered, and candles flickered on the long tables. There was no set dress code, but members had made an effort to turn out in their finest clothes. The Master of Ceremonies, Association President Rache Murphy, stood at a podium at one end of the room, flicking through his notes and murmuring into his microphone.

"I can definitely see it getting into the newsletter," Lewis Begley whispered. He was the editor of the Association's *Enigmatic Imaginings Quarterly*, and had endured many pleas from Crawford to disperse his work.

"Could you? That'd be grand." Crawford shuffled his photos away and sipped his coffee. "Don't suppose you'd know what the others have got."

"Nothing to do with me. I'm not on the committee. I know Grueb had been talking about his expedition to Isla de la Muñecas again."

"…a far finer gathering has never…" Murphy muttered under his breath, or what would have been under his breath had the microphone not been on. "Er, for the bravery to face corruption…"

"Fuck, is he still spouting that rubbish?"

"Oh, he's doing a whole paper on it now. He says the use of dolls to communicate with the unseen goes back centuries, not just with the island. Ushabti, voodoo dolls, homunculi as a vessel to allow the unseen a physical presence, that kind of thing."

"He's going on about possession now? Lovely."

"Nah, I don't think he wants to quite suggest that. As I understand it, the idea is more that the human shape makes perceptible ripples to unseen senses. Or something." He shrugged. "Bit beyond me. Have you been to Kampung Monyet? It's a slum in Jakarta where the locals dress up macaques in kiddie clothes and masks to dance for money. But Grueb was saying he had it on good authority there were groups interpreting their dances as reactions to attracted unseen."

Crawford laughed, shook his head. "There's nothing to suggest that the unseen can even perceive us, let alone touch us."

"Yeah, I know. It's gonna get quite divisive whenever he decides to publish. Might just bring up the whole 'poltergeist activity' argument again."

There was a gasp from the dais. "Yes! Er. Could I just have everyone's attention now? We are ready to begin."

Most of the audience was already listening, having followed his amplified whispers. Murphy gulped at the assembled eyes gazing back at him and steadied himself on the podium.

"Ah, ladies and gentlemen. It is my. Pleasure to welcome you once again to the one-hundred-and-twelfth Photo Competition of the Association of Seekers of the Great Unseen!" He finished in a strangled wheeze, but his features dissolved to gratification as the audience applauded. It was a dutiful, mechanical applause; nobody came for the ceremony, or the niceties. They came to outdo one another, and to see others outdone.

"As you all know, tonight we will review the finalists submitted to the awards committee, after weeks of careful consideration and review was granted to the many others. I must say there, er, were quite a lot of brilliant snapshots shown to us this year. But alas! Er, alas, we have only five awards to offer, and only four will be selected."

"Surprised you've not tried this year, Paul," Scageson said. "You've been with us two years. And I know you've got a few good shots squirreled away somewhere."

He did, to show himself willing; and sometimes it was only the knowledge of his unfair advantage that kept him from blowing his cover. He shrugged, smiled sheepishly.

"Nah, I'm still learning."

"Good lad!" Crawford's laughter caused several starts, including Murphy's. "Know your limitations, that's what I'm told."

Now Murphy was beginning to lose his short-lived relief.

"Categories!" he squeaked. "Categories are…are…categories are. Greatest Clarity. Rarity of Subject. And…and Personal Danger. And of course, the greatest photograph that has been seen to meet all of these criteria shall…shall receive the Year Achievement Award!" Murphy looked as if he expected applause to erupt at this. It did not. "Ah. Let us begin. With Greatest Clarity."

He pulled down a screen. The projectionist switched his machine to flickering life. Greenish-gray light filled the screen.

"Nominees are…Caleb Vale!"

A dark-skinned man in thick-rimmed glasses smiled thinly at the desultory applause.

"Taylor Calder!"

"Why don't they show us the photos they took?" Lieson whispered as the names were recited

"Club rules. Only the winning photo gets shown. Saves time that way." Crawford shrugged. "Besides, they'll get into the newsletter anyway, and nobody really cares. It's only the winner that matters."

"The winner! Ah. The winner is! Ethan Steele!"

"All right!" A broad-shouldered man leapt up from his table, whooping and punching the air. The applause this time may have been very nearly genuine. The projectionist placed a slide into the machine.

An image appeared on the screen. Paul managed to disguise his gasp as a hasty cough. The woman was naked, and her eyes were hooded. She was obviously drugged, and bound to the bed with thin nylon rope.

The most shocking thing, however, was the creature squatting over her like an eager lover; Lieson was reminded of Fuseli's *Nightmare*. It was almost humanoid; its limbs were absurdly long and thin, and slightly blurry, as the thing was caught in mid-movement. Its head was a pale coconut, completely bare, the back of it shown to the camera as it leaned over the woman.

Scages gave a low whistle. "Clearest I've ever seen a leering tom. Never knew they were so skinny."

"Must have been hell to photograph," Begley said. "They move so fast you're lucky to catch it capering. Camera must've been on repeat flash. Damned clever."

Crawford groaned. "He laid a damn trap for the thing! I call that cheating."

"Nothing in the rules against it, Benji. It's just common sense."

Lieson gaped at the others. "You're saying he got that woman, and…"

The three seasoned members laughed at his disbelieving expression.

"She's just tied up, mate. Not as if she's lying dead in an alley."

"Yes, but—"

"Probably paid off well for her, I shouldn't wonder. Steele's a straight-enough lad."

"Don't let it worry you."

"Straight, my arse."

Lieson stared at the woman in the photo. Of course, he'd known the Association attracted those with a blasé attitude towards unsavory activities. It stood to reason—if you couldn't face the visible horrors, you had no hope of seeing the invisible ones. Even so, the idea that they might take a more proactive approach to the game to attract their quarry left a queasy feeling in his stomach.

The woman looked as if she had bruises on her shoulders, but before Lieson could ask the photo was removed from the projector.

"And now, our nominees for, um, Rarity…"

"What category did you try for, Benji?"

"All of them, of course. I figured mine covered all the bases. Clear pic in a crime scene of an unseen that's only found in places of prolonged sexual abuse that occur in the *countryside*. Take it from me, it don't get trickier than that." Crawford's cheeks were beginning to redden. He was on his fourth glass of champagne. His eyes were riveted to the stage.

"You must have had a good lead, though. I mean, once the writher's there it's not tricky to find. It'll lie there gorging itself for weeks. But you had to *know* it would be there.

"Yeah," Scageson whispered. "Whatcha use? Police scanner? Contacts?"

"Oh, this and that, boys, this and that."

Lieson studied Crawford. If the man had contacts they'd likely been found by now. Fresh constables, the occasional examiner—anyone you'd expect to be on the scene for a while. None of them had been particularly imaginative. It was all the same to them if some loony wanted to see where somebody was murdered, so long as they had ready money.

"James Sykes!"

Crawford groaned. "Oh, that fucking prig..."

Sykes, a portly man in glasses with short, silvery hair, shook the Murphy's hand warmly and smiled to the audience as he accepted his award.

"Lotta piss in that one," Begley said. "Bigshot American lawyer. Filthy rich. Dunno why he bothers with all this, all the money he's got."

"Never could stand him," Scageson agreed. "He's always going on about knowing statesmen and celebrities and that. Heard he's got his own plane as well."

At first, the photo appeared to be a clear expanse of cloudy white. Then, Lieson realized the photo *was* clouds—an overcast sky.

Sykes nudged Murphy away from the podium. "This was taken over the South China Sea," he said. From his pocket he produced a pointer and extended it. "I realize it may be difficult to make out, but if you look in the upper left corner of the photograph..." He tapped the screen. "...you will see a thin, hemispherical shape. If you observe *here* and *here*, you will see what are almost certainly vast, diaphanous wings. And here, I believe, is its proboscis."

Lieson squinted. With difficulty, he could see a sort of dark blot against the clouds, but it seemed far too small to determine its shape.

"The existence of the *buteo ejecter*, or skyjacker's buzzard, has never been officially determined by the Association. It was during my own investigation of the possible site of the recent disappearance—"

"Foul!" Crawford bellowed from the table, making rude gestures towards the stage. "Fucking foul!"

The shout was taken across the room, as well as cries of "You can't see anything!" and "He's having your lady behind your back, Murphy!"

"Gentlemen! Ah, please!" Murphy's ineffectual admonitions were ignored by the assembled membership. Sykes glared at the catcalls and taunts. Then folded his pointer and picked up his award before leaving the stage and fleeing the room with as much dignity as he could manage.

"Christ, Benji, it's just a prize when all's said and done—" Bengley began.

"Oh, lighten up," Scageson replied. "Sykes does this with every bloody contest. He can't win by actual skill, so he's gotta win on technicalities. And he *is* having Murphy's wife."

"Well, that's no story. He screws everyone's wife."

Crawford had scarcely drained his glass before he began refilling it. Lieson stared at him as he fumbled the bottle, spilling quite a lot of it.

"What?" he snapped.

"Is there such a thing as a skyjacker's buzzard?"

Crawford slugged down the glassful breathlessly. "Sykes' just having us on."

"So, you don't know if it's real or not?"

"Christ, Paul, what're you on about? It's never been seen, never been observed. It's just like Sykes to try and say a blimp or something's the buzzard. Such a goddamn blowhard."

"But if it was real," Lieson persisted. "If it was, then you could find missing planes, right? I dunno how long it'd hang about, but if you used the membrane cameras to track it…"

"Oh, that's an interesting thought!" Scageson said, trying to lighten the mood. "Eh, Benji? You'd be like a detective, solving unsolved mysteries."

Crawford glared at them over his glass, a little unsteadily. "It's daft."

Bengley leaned over to Lieson. "Never seen him in such a mood. He's never been what you'd call a good sport, but he's taken the contests in his stride, till now."

"Maybe we ought to get the bottle away from him, do you think?"

"You're welcome to try."

Like a shaken card shark, Crawford shuffled his photos, holding them before his face as if to hide his expression. Lieson could hear him muttering "Should have tried the clinger, should have tried..."

"Our final category! Our most prestigious distinction! Personal Danger! Nominees..."

"They don't know the half of it, they don't..."

"What's that, Benji?"

"Never you mind. Where's that bottle?"

"You dropped it."

"Damn! Someone get me another."

It was nearly impossible to make out the names of the nominees through Murphy's stuttering. Across the lounge, the assembled Association tittered with false starts.

"Benji, this could be it, eh? You don't want to be too drunk for the acceptance speech."

"Fuck the speech." Crawford's fought to get the words out, the scotch doing for him what stage fright was doing to Murphy. "It's all dross, anyway. I know I'm good, right? I know I'm good!"

"Octavius Killinger!"

"*Fuck you!*" Crawford gripped the table and tried to lift it. Unfortunately, his mind was not in an ideal state, and he succeeded only in launching off the table as if it were a springboard and collapsing onto the floor.

"Fuck. Fuck it." Crawford waved away proffered hands, clutching his photos to his sizable chest. "No fucking appreciation, none at all."

Like a portly pinball Crawford staggered through the lounge, bouncing back and forth off each shocked and indignant table, slurring curses and insults to all.

An hour later, most of the tables were vacated. The stragglers gravitated to Lieson's table, including the Association president, who was sipping cautiously at a large glass of water.

"I'm...I'm sure many tempers were rather frayed this year," he murmured.

"It's no excuse," Bengley said. "There was no call getting so cross. And drinking so much! You ask me, we should put him right out."

"I suppose he just felt a bit cheated," Lieson said. "He must have put a lot of effort into getting that photo."

"So what? We all do. It's not like birdwatching. You don't just wait for hours in the field trying to spot a speckled warbler or whatever." Scageson dragged his cigarette down to a stub, then crumbled the ashes onto his plate. "We all take risks. He knows that."

"And it's not like it matters, anyway," Bengley said. "There's always next year. We all have our go. There's always opportunities."

Murphy took a deep breath, tried to speak as slowly and clearly as possible. "Yes. And that's why it's…rather disappointing. You see. Um. You see. There was another award."

"*Another* award?"

"Yes. It's…it's new. A Lifetime Achievement sort of thing. The committee decided that photo warranted it."

"Whose? Crawford's?"

"Yes! That's why it's so upsetting, you see. We thought it'd be an excellent way to recognize his efforts. He's been trying for so many years, you know. Frankly, he's the most remarkable spotter in decades. We were even thinking about a portrait. Perhaps even naming a room after him."

Scageson leaned back and laughed uproariously. Bengley narrowed his eyes.

"I don't believe it! You're gonna give that arrogant bastard everything he's ever wanted?"

"Were," Lieson corrected him. "I just hope he won't be too hungover tomorrow."

"Well I…I suppose we could mail it to him. It'll be rather difficult. He does seem to move around a lot. I've no idea where he's living now."

"What's his last-known address? Maybe we could start there."

"Somewhere in Bath, I believe. Ex-excuse me, gentlemen, I need a lie-down, I think."

Paul Lieson left the lounge of the Great Unseen Association behind. It was not quite a confirmation, but it was good as any he was likely to get. He removed the recorder secured in his tie. The next morning would find the Association's headquarters swarming with policemen overturning boxes, rifling through drawers and files and photographs of invisible creatures squatting over visible atrocities. No doubt years of unsolved disappearances would be settled in short order.

And if I have anything to say about it, Detective Inspector Paul Lieson thought, *we'll send some special cameras the way of Missing Persons.*

THE MEEK

"Charity," said the homeless man, *"is, by definition, an abom-*inable act."

He had a refined sort of voice, if a little rough. I imagined he must have been a smoker once; his skin was leathery, with an orangeish tinge. His teeth were yellow, and his red beard was spotted with what might have been ash.

I'd met him standing along a grassy verge next to the stop-light by the highway exit, holding a cardboard sign that said HUNGRY AND HOMELESS. PLEASE HELP AND GOD BLESS.

Homeless people worry me. I look away when I end up next to them, counting the seconds under my breath until the light changes. I used to give them money, until a friend shamed me for it.

An old man in a dirty brown coat had asked us if we could spare some change for the bus. I gave him a tenner, mostly just to get rid of him. My friend gave me a hard time anyway.

"He's down here every night," he told me. "And I've never seen him at a bus stop. You're too trusting."

I wasn't, really. It just seemed easier to give them money than not. Perhaps there was a part of me that felt sorry for them; but it was a small part, and it only got smaller as time went on. The strength to look away was never something that came easily to me; I've always preferred the path of least resistance.

I tried not to notice the man on the verge by the stoplight, but there seemed to be no way to do that without being obvious. I couldn't stop myself from glancing at him and, by accident, catching his eye. I thought for maybe half a second before I rolled down my window and called him over.

"You hungry?"

I was surprised how young he looked beneath his beard; slight laugh lines creased his face.

"I surely am."

"Hop in."

I took him to a good deli I knew, ordered roast beef sandwiches and coffee for us both. The waitress looked as if she wanted to protest but kept quiet.

"My god, does it feel good to sit in a real chair," sighed the homeless man. "You don't realize how hard the damn street is till you sleep on it every night."

Some of the other customers were giving us strange looks. I tried not to notice.

"How long have you been living like this?"

"Couple months, I think. Maybe longer. I've never been great at keeping track of time, even before my fall from grace." He sipped his coffee. "Not that I was ever much of an angel."

"What did you do?"

"I was sort of an academic. Kept my head up in the clouds and down in the books, for all the good it's done me."

"You were a professor?"

He smiled, and tilted his head. "They don't look too happy, do they?" He pointed to a table in the corner, where a woman was shooting sideways glances at us. The man was staring down at his food in a deliberate manner. "We must be making them nervous."

"Why would we make them nervous?"

"Me, because I'm a homeless bum and probably a criminal. You, because you're with me."

"*Are* you a criminal?"

"Maybe to some people. No matter what you do, there's always somebody who frowns on it."

"We can leave if they're upsetting you."

"Not at all. Just making a point." He bit into his sandwich, chewing slowly with a look of utter satisfaction.

"What was your subject?" I didn't want to pry too deeply, but I was curious. "Sociology?"

"Hm. Folklore, I suppose. Old stories, forgotten habits. Old stuff."

I couldn't stop myself now. "What sort of old stuff?"

He grinned; bits of meat were caught in his teeth. "You really wanna hear it?"

"Please. It sounds fascinating."

He sat up a little straighter. His hands folded over the table-top. There was a dignity in him that went beyond the solemnity of a beggar. I had no trouble seeing him as a respected university man.

"People fear otherness," he explained. "It speaks to the heart of our protective and competitive spirits. We need to protect our children and our property, and we need somebody to feel superior to. It probably goes all the way back to the cave, and I believe it is why so much of our literature—and our other arts, for that matter—has gone towards depicting inhuman things that have preyed on us by exploiting our sense of charity."

"Really?"

"Oh, yes, although it has often varied as to who gave and who received. The classic example would be the stories of mortals making deals with demonic entities—blues singers at crossroads and so on. The stigma is usually placed on the greed that drove such exchanges, but I believed it was the notion of parley with the inhuman other that truly offended."

None of my own professors had spoken so eloquently; he seemed an academic of the old school, an anachronism of an educator.

"Eve and the serpent."

"Precisely, yes. Among other examples beyond the biblical, Persephone could not leave Hades once she had eaten fruit from the Underworld; and it is generally advisable to not eat the food in Faerie—what you might call Fairyland—nor to accept any gifts from the fair folk."

"Why's that?"

"Because you would be obliged to serve them for hundreds of years, usually. Although their beauty was supposedly such that many might find the prospect enjoyable.

"Or there were the more obviously malicious creatures, such as the kelpie—water horses that enticed the unwary into climbing on and riding them, and then bolting to the nearest lake to drown them."

"Wait," I said. "So, somebody sees a random horse kinda loitering on the shore and decides to ride it?"

He laughed. "That's how it went. And the sirens! Pretty ladies sunning themselves and singing to the sailors to come and crash their boats upon the rocks." He wiped his mouth with a napkin, took a noisy slurp of coffee. "All of this trickery, this exploitation of human curiosity. All of it taken in, where does that leave us?"

I shrugged, too interested to speak.

"It left *me* thinking that these creatures were operating from a position of weakness, and had to use whatever talents they could muster to get their prey to do the hard work for them. No vampire walked through a door uninvited. The danger is perfectly surmountable, so long as one does not give into their fascination."

The waitress brought our check. I fished out my wallet.

"But these things have supernatural powers, don't they? Strength, or…"

He shook his head ruefully. "Overinflated peasant tales. These things are weak, you may depend on it. Their strength lies in the superficial. Beauty, or the promise of wealth and knowledge. All glamour. And that, I think, is why people worry about giving too freely, in case there is a price they don't know about just waiting to spring up. Charity is an abominable act."

——

The chill had picked up outside. This was the worst of the winter, and I could see the homeless man was discomfited by it.

"Thank you so much for the meal, friend." His voice was tight, as if he was trying to keep his teeth from chattering.

I couldn't stop myself; now that I'd begun, it seemed heartless not to go further.

"Do you need a place to sleep tonight?"

The look of gratitude on his face nearly brought tears to my eyes. He lit up immeasurably, and was all smiles as we got back to my car.

"What was it that got you into that stuff? Monsters and that?"

He hissed thoughtfully through his teeth. "I suppose you could say heredity. Or heritage."

My knuckles grew stiff on the steering wheel; it turned against my volition. My feet moved over the pedals. I was cold with sweat, although the heater was blowing at full blast.

"Weakness," he breathed. "That is the great distinction. Medusa could not look on another living soul. The Minotaur could never be free from his maze. Vampires would never know warmth, werewolves peace of mind. The serpent was made to crawl upon the ground."

A sweet, metallic smell filled the car. My eyes stayed on the road; I couldn't turn my head. In my peripheral vision, it seemed as if the homeless academic were wriggling very slightly.

"I can only imagine there was some great transgression in the past, some act so unspeakable the souls responsible would be punished forevermore, throughout history, endlessly incarnating in ever more horrid forms, each one crippled in some fundamental way. Yet they always managed to make their weakness work for them. They embraced it, and used it to go on.

"Because men are curious. There will always be someone to look back at the crumbling city. To go walking of an evening under the full moon, to open the casket, to spend the night in the haunted house."

His hand grasped mine. The skin was coarse and leathery, and I could feel very fine hairs.

"Maybe if they stopped being...what they were, eh? Just stopped acting like monsters. That would be a grand, cosmic irony, wouldn't it? Refuse to bite, or just drive the stake through your own heart. Maybe that would end the cycle.

"But perhaps they don't want to end it. Habit, maybe. Or just having come to like it. Better to reign in hell, and all that. You can't tell me Lucifer didn't do what he did without knowing he might fall."

We turned onto my street. I felt like I was in a dream, utterly gripped with fear but unable to do anything about it.

"Well, never mind," he said cheerfully. "I'm still looking. Things will come round again."

He got out of the car, strolled over to my side. By the time I thought to make a run for it he had already opened the door.

"And in the meantime, there's plenty to do." His voice was harsh, and deep.

There was a natural rapport between the disconnected, but D'shall knew it was almost always a pointless endeavor. Those who abandoned the world and derided it as frivolous told themselves there was a truer world to join, and became as insular as suicide cultists. Then, they turned to the arts, and dabbled in music or sculpture or writing, thinking it would be enough. But, sooner or later, they realized the long road to making something of it and lost their nerve.

Those moping bastards he'd used to humor in pubs and coffee shops, feigning interest in their unrealized ideas and works in indefinite progress. What would they make of this place? If they knew its story, they might label it an escape for inspiration. They tended towards the superstitious, and preached unashamedly of their favored pens and arranged corners of solitude. They could make a Mecca of this place, where so many of their kind came to wallow and consider themselves virtuous.

There again, it might be a hell to them. The lazy creatures hated anything that stank of regulation. They were at home with their own pain, out of sight of all but the imagined leers and jibing grins they applied to outsiders, but in actual company it somehow became too much to bear. However romanticized the suffering in the Library had been expressed in the pamphlet, even the memory of it might keep them away.

Suited him fine. If D'shall could come back he would take a match to the place. He'd yet to see a sign of those sentinel wraiths. They were hardly there to begin with; perhaps they evaporated completely once their job was done.

But there was still the old woman. Her visit to his room was more dream than anything else, but D'shall had no doubt she was tucked away somewhere.

He still had the makeshift knife in his coat. Her monsters would not take the manuscript from him easily. He read on.

SICKNESS IS FLESH

Word was sent to the yellow woman in the whispery, ephemer-
al way of the twilight world—the Lady of Limbs required her
services.

She was being kept in the private ward of the Geneviève Kathlier Private Hospital, occupied by long-term patients. These were
people sick for so long they could not imagine any other state.
Their health stumbled in fits and starts, and it was never certain if
they would live to feel another heartbeat, let alone see another day.
Their families, generally wealthy and yet short on compassion, left
them to the ministrations of the greatest help money could buy and
put them out of mind.

The yellow woman was kept in a locked, windowless ward.
The only person who had a key was a young nurse, and she rarely
had occasion to think about it. Nobody else knew about that ward,
not even the head physician.

The Lady had passed the job on to her directly. One day Her
men came, in their red leather suits and featureless red helmets,
carrying between them the limp, moaning form of the young
nurse's brother. He owed a debt he had no means of paying.

The nurse did not ask for details, but immediately offered to
do whatever was needed to make things right.

She didn't see her brother anymore after that, but the duty remained.

Since then, she had been required to wake the yellow woman only twice. The first time, she did the job quickly and ran from the room without looking back. The second time, she'd steeled her nerves to stay. Only when the form rose from the bed and the eyes like scarlet neon pierced the darkness did she give in and flee.

This new message came just as mysteriously as any other—in a bottle of formaldehyde, imprinted on something fleshy and organic, best not to speculate what. The Lady's mark, a curling tentacle that wavered suggestively in the murky fluid, was carved into it; and the nurse again felt the littlest nibble of the unnamable emotion—something between dread and excitement, for the two are never quite separate. She could not refuse the job, she knew that much. The end would likely come when she least expected it, when her flesh betrayed her without a whisper.

Down to the secret ward she went; it looked for all the world like a broom closet from the outside. Nothing, not the faintest hum, marked it as something extraordinary. The nurse unlocked it hurriedly and ducked inside before she could be seen.

It was a tiny cell, made tinier by the banks of machinery that kept the yellow woman sleeping. A large bank of electronic buttons gleamed black in the unlit room. The only illumination was the glow of the yellow lady herself—a sickly jaundiced light from her feverish skin. She lay, asleep, in her sealed glass sarcophagus.

There was a sheaf of papers on a shelf. The nurse picked it up and flicked to the relevant page. Even though she was sure she could do it from memory if necessary, she preferred not to take chances. There were many buttons, and the thought of anything going wrong filled her with dread.

She read the passwords and protocols. She read them again, following with her finger and mouthing the characters to herself silently. With painful slowness, she typed them in, keeping the papers open in front of her and watching them as she typed.

A pause. Two. Then, she pressed the final key.

A beeping countdown. The nurse backed away, shaking terribly, her eyes riveted to the sarcophagus. A hiss of decompressing air, and the glow of flesh intensified. Eyes snapped open—siren red, without iris or pupil.

Wiry hair crackled like static as the yellow woman sat up. Tubes snapped off fleshy gauges in her arms. The yellow light of her skin made it difficult to determine her facial features; the faintest smudges of shadow might have delineated the general vicinity of her mouth and nose. In truth, her face was a living, mucus-colored swirl, her expressions causing the color to shimmer and waver.

Her voice was plague and hay fever; black-lunged air whispered over a tongue lined with silver, and through teeth red as passion.

"Well?"

The nurse, crouched in a corner behind the machinery, emerged hesitantly, and held out the jar. Lemon-lime hands snatched it away and unscrewed the lid.

The yellow woman regarded the jagged marks on the preserved organ—something like a kidney, or a liver.

"Ah, yes," she breathed. "Yes." She opened her mouth, wide as a serpent's, and carefully slid the organ into her mouth, savoring it before swallowing.

Neurotransmitters fizzed into new pathways. Succulent chemicals surged and roiled. Information transcribed into protein combinations arrived so abruptly into her mind that the yellow woman gasped, her glow flashing for a few wild moments as the nurse watched on, disgusted and terrified.

She knew a name, and a list of addresses. She had instructions.

"Get on with it," she said.

The nurse edged out of the room and closed the door. As she did so, every light in the hospital went out. Auxiliary power had only been on for a moment when the mains were restored. In that moment, a sickly glow might have been seen, like an optical illusion caused by the change of light, but nobody commented on it.

※

The Lady of Limbs has held the stars in her hands, and the soil. She has dug her fingers into the membranes of dreaming corpses and the eyes of feverish vapors. From all things that are, she weaves tapestries of flesh and dust that scream in saline fumes, and figures draped in taste and touch to caress the brows of sweaty insomniacs.

153

Strictly speaking, she has no need for hired violence. Oh, she has her red-suited men, but they could more properly be thought of as couriers, only occasionally called upon to deliver menace.

The Lady flourishes in the halls of the mighty and the influential. Anyone who thinks they might abuse her services or leave debts unpaid has nobody to turn to—not their friends, who were as likely in her grip, nor the police, who do not go in for the outlandish. As it is she takes care to know far, far more about her clients than they will ever know of her. It tends to do the trick.

But there are problems, and then there were the problems that flatly refuse to be solved by conventional methods. Unexpectedly resourceful problems, with places and identities to pick up as the need arose, and the willingness to do so. That is a rare development in her world, where the mighty and influential, in the face of impending implosion, dither and make empty threats, trying to outstare the oncoming lights and refusing to run. A clever client is an unforeseen and unwelcome surprise.

So, the Lady of Limbs, in her tangential ways, tinkers and devises and ponders and digs her innumerable tentacles and finds a solution, pleasingly, take shape. She will have no run-of-the-mill killer—no, not some thug of the streets. For pride and aesthetics, she will make her own.

It was not difficult; her clients paid to be deified, made inhuman. But with the change in appearance there had to be a change in structure, else the body would collapse. Bones must be strengthened, limbs tightened, muscles bulked. Chemical cocktails had to be synthesized and adapted for the system. The result was that even the least modified of the Lady's clients were quite capable of feats of destruction, if the thought ever entered their vain little minds.

Of course, there were safeguards in the unlikely event that they did, because the Lady is no fool. It should not have been possible for anyone to toy with her without finding their brains filled with steaming alkaline and their muscles seizing into piercing needles.

This time, however,, a more proactive approach was called for.

The yellow woman knew this—we are born dying. From the day she first fell, screaming, from between her mother's legs onto the cold city filth, she knew that she rocked on the edge of oblivion. That was the knowledge she carried from her first day, and it was that alone which allowed her to survive.

The streets are unforgiving, whether you are born to them or you are driven to them. It does not matter—you are a street thing now, and anything you take will be taken back. Anything given away will not be replaced. There is no morality in the alleys where there is nobody to see. Children learn this, or they die. It is the only education that counts.

This child was cannier than most. From birth, she'd been passed among the destitute like an heirloom, raised more or less by accident. Childless mothers are mothers nonetheless, and although each met her own unfortunate end she saw to it the girl received some semblance of an upbringing.

The girl, against all likelihood, lived and grew, and learned early on how to be appealing enough to care for. She would appear in the homeless camps, a filthy child in ragged clothes yet possessed of a fierce loveliness the downtrodden could not reject. She was a beautiful thing; she was *their* beautiful thing.

When this was reported to the Lady of Limbs, she was fascinated. The streets were not unknown to her; she had been born on them—or under them, rather—after all. She utilized them as the need came. She could always find a use for spare flesh, spare blood. This girl was a wonder, a predator in a sea of meek little fishes. A girl to watch.

And watch the Lady did. She watched the child grow into a young woman—a queen, in her way. She never tried to raise herself up from the gutter, not when there were so many willing to care for her. She seldom had to beg herself. The others would share their food with her, their takings, their less-worn clothing, their space. She was treasured.

It is a mystery, then, why she did not resist when the Lady sent the red-suited men to fetch her. Her guardians did, sure enough. They charged, screaming, from the tenement doors, some carrying pipes, some carrying broken bottles and bags of bricks, most resorting to their hands to claw and punch. They'd had no forewarning, no intelligence. They just saw the red-suited men and knew immediately what they'd come for.

Uncomplicated people would have found the resistance terrifying, but the red-suited men were certainly complicated. They were not men, and never had been. They absorbed the blows, stretched pliantly as the hands sought purchase. They moved like latex, sinuously weaving between their opponents, pulling themselves out of the way of every cut and thrust. Quicker than blinking, they whipped round bodies and crushed the life out of them like man-shaped boa constrictors, poured arms down throats until they burst and the lungs stopped breathing.

The girl—the woman—did not run nor resist the red-suited men, who found her reclining in the largest, cushiest pile of rags. She knew the streets better than anyone, and they shared their whispers with her more readily than could be known. These liquid assailants were no strange thing to her, nor did she doubt for one moment there were stranger things by far. We are born dying, so the only thing to do is bide our time until the end, or until we become undying.

<hr />

The man's name was Gamberly, a self-made magnate, although that was less impressive than it used to be. Media, marketing, electronic entertainment—it was all the same to the Lady what the man did. She had people who kept tabs on his work. The yellow woman knew everything they'd compiled—his addresses, his known associates, his corporate holdings, his BMI. It all sat in her mind, and she could call up any of it as she pleased.

Gamberly's modifications were largely internal, but extensive; by all accounts, it was the Lady's greatest work yet. Gamberly could move his veins at will as if his skin were alive with mobile calligraphy. His nerves buzzed with a subtle, pleasurable current that showed in his lazy smile.

Arrogance showed, as well, which is why it was not entirely surprising that he would attempt to escape without paying. What *was* surprising, however, was that he'd somehow managed it. The red-suited men placed to guard him were found as limp, red skins marked by a single, tiny puncture. Of Gamberly there was no sign.

The Lady was furious, then intrigued, and then furious again. The skins were processed, as were a few members of her staff. Suitably calmed, she sent word for her last safeguard. It was when they thought they were clever that people most amused her, but the fun had to run its course eventually.

The yellow woman slithered like an aurora through the sleeping streets. She moved in a streak of ball lightning, a sphere of color in the flash of a camera phone, a flock of buzzing points in a cone of streetlight. She relied on the blink of sight from walking out of the shadows—not the absence of light but its passage, or arrival; that microsecond as it chased away the darkness and the eyes, for only a moment, do not know where they are.

Her primary objective was to eliminate the threat; but secondary to that was to discover, if possible, the source of Gamberly's protections. Whatever solution he'd used to deflate the red-suited men suggested a knowledge not dissimilar to the Lady's own, but the disabling of the remote aneurisms planted in his head was truly worrisome. It was nothing for which the Lady could not prepare, if necessary; but she could not countenance the knowledge in a human head. There could be no equals; flesh was *her* canvas.

A moment of cellular buzzing—synaptic communication— and the yellow woman had a possible lead—Adrian Testel, a plastic surgeon of little repute who operated in the Yeoman district and was a known associate of Gamberly's. The man's operation was just short of *dis*reputable, and the only reason he hadn't been sued for malpractice a hundred times over was because of extensive legal aid provided by a firm that also represented Gamberly.

It was enough. The silent haze of the yellow woman spat and crackled through bulbs and wires, deep into the Yeoman district.

⁂

To become an undying thing, concessions must be made. Death must be courted respectfully to gain its favors. For all that she claimed dominion over human anatomy, the Lady was careful to maintain balance. New additions needed to be secured— shafts of marrow were propped, blood vessels required additional passages. Concessions were needed between the marriage of skin and scale, feather and hair, teeth and tongue. This is why the Lady conserved every spare bit she could.

Almost nothing of the yellow woman was entirely her own. The human frame is malleable in ways few understand, but it has its limitations. It simply is not built to hold such a multitude of caustic substances, to be a living assassination factory. We are born dying. The yellow woman had needed to be made dead.

Even before the candidate was selected, the Lady of Limbs worked many months to create the perfect vessel. All other operations were put on hold. Agents were recalled, facilities were reassigned. New compounds needed to be synthesized, spare material concentrated into this most ambitious project.

Much of this was applied to the Lady herself. Centuries of accumulated biomass provided her with only a few of the tools necessary. Inorganic components were needed if the project was to work. Ingots of tungsten and iron and molybdenum were brought to her. Mad glasswork spiraled into her pit, all of it sampled. Let it not be said that the Lady of Limbs was not prepared to learn.

The body was a stiff plastic shell with artificial veins. No stomach—the creature would not eat. No lungs—the creature would not breathe. It would draw its life from toxic substances. In every way, it would embrace death.

The young woman was eager. She could not stop staring at the vessel all through the procedure.

"You will be as fire," said the Lady's aide, a pale, thin woman with hair like dead branches curving about her head. "You will be as light. Subtlety is not what she expects. You must inspire fear. You must inspire dread. You must make it clear to anyone who dares defy her the dreadful error they have made. Understand?"

She did. Raising her arms, the young woman was lifted into the sinewy embrace of the Lady. She gasped with pleasure as the needles dug into her brain, and rejoiced in the delicious rush as the light faded from her eyes at last.

The Yeoman district lay at the outskirts of the city, hugging Goria's crumbling stone walls. It had been an over-large series of barracks for the city's defenders, who had been renowned for the fervor with which they both pursued their duty and looked after their own affairs. It was said they had been too paranoid to differentiate much between friend and foe; so, like much of everything else, the Gorian Guard Corps decayed save for a few ragged pockets of traditionalists rabid with imagined duties, jumpy at the least provocation, letting off flocks of ancient arrows at anything that moved.

It would be a desperate sort of businessman to do his business there; they were just as likely to die, after all, as anyone to come looking for them.

Many of the streetlights were in disrepair. The yellow woman was unconcerned; she shone like a beacon in the gloom, but she knew nobody would be fool enough to approach her. The area's inhabitants had learned to react in a certain way to approaching lights of any kind; the darkness was their truest friend.

Testel's practice was located in a disused water treatment plant; the yellow woman had no doubt he made ready use of the pumps in disposing of waste. The sewers rumbled all hours. A lot got flushed away in Goria.

A single light flickered over the front door—brand-new steel, tall and thick, with security cameras on either side. Gamberly's work, without question.

The yellow woman paused. In situations like this, she would normally try for a back route. However, the plant was a large place, and the fact that so much effort had been expended on this entrance told her the action could not be far off. In any event, she was not designed for stealthy assassination. She was an apparition, sensational and otherworldly. They needed to see.

The woman tensed on the edge of the shadows. Charges sparked over her flesh, vessels contracted. Then, she *leapt*...

The guard was pitiably old, for all his military bearing and close-cropped hair. To his credit, he did not hesitate to investigate the blackout following the intense light. He shined his torch into the pool of shadow, and had only a moment to perceive the vague glow before she was on him like a lightning bolt.

The yellow woman's hair came to life like Medusa's snakes. Spear-tipped wires buried themselves into the guard's face. A moment's struggle before the toxins flushed his system, and it was over.

She withdrew, fighting the impulse to collapse. Her body had been designed to utilize inorganic poisons in much the same manner as blood. It taxed her to lose even a small amount. Her body would eventually replenish what it had lost; but until she was safely ensconced back at the Kathlier, she must take it slow.

No need for stealth now. The woman walked calmly through the door and proceeded down the dimly lit hallway. As she'd suspected, Testel, and presumably Gamberly, were not far: she could see brighter light around the edges of a door to her right. It was enough; she became haze, seeped through the cracks, and reconstituted on the other side.

It had once been a locker room. Most of the space had been cleared to make way for jerry-rigged lab equipment—EKGs, stretchers, great messy cables crowding in the corners. A fat man with peppery gray hair—Testel—was shaking badly enough to cause the desk he hid under to clatter. With casual strength, she tugged him out and held him to the floor.

"He made me do it!" he shrieked. He smelled disgusting, and his coat was covered in reddish-brown stains. "I gave him the solvent and he told me to cut the thing out of his head and I told him I didn't know brains but he insisted!" Testel babbled desperately, apparently less fazed by the sight of the yellow woman than by what she meant to do to him.

The yellow woman said nothing; she raised her hairs thoughtfully and held them just above the skin of his face.

"No, please! I can tell you everything! He wanted the veins to enhance the drugs. I told him there'd be consequences but he was so certain. I worship the Lady of Limbs! I've seen her work from afar. But something's gone wrong! He made me violate her art. I didn't want to, I swear I didn't want to…"

Very gently, she plugged the hairs into his face. He squealed as the poisons dumped into his system.

There was a crash from behind. A bed the yellow woman had not noticed had toppled to the floor with its thrashing occupant. Gamberly was nude and pale. His flesh rippled like an ocean stirred by a storm. His teeth were clenched, his fingers digging grooves into the floor tiles.

Facial features formed and faded. His eyes disappeared in melted flesh, reappeared, disappeared again. The scent of chemicals was ripe on the air; an unnatural white substance clung to his inner thighs, and congealed on the overturned sheets.

The yellow woman kicked Testel aside. It seemed her business would sort itself out; Gamberly was not long for this life. No sense in wasting her poisons on him.

However…

She examined the dried ichor. It smelt of burning plastics, of meth, and something of steroids. Testel's homegrown narcotics. A super-drug. Gamberly must have believed the motility of his veins would enhance the effect. Idiot.

Her hairs slurped up the remains. The Lady was always willing to learn something new.

There was no need to dispose of the bodies in the Yeoman district. The glowing specter walked into the night.

THE BLACK SQUIRREL

If you've found this, then you're probably an ambulance work-
er. Or a cop. You'll think this is my suicide note.

I suppose it is. But it is also my confession.

Believe me when I say I don't want to do this. I've been pushed
to it, but not by the university. It's not their fault. I have no choice;
worse things will happen if I don't go through with this. I don't
like to think what they'll do.

I admit I was a terrible student. I took on too much, and got
upset when I couldn't pull through it on time. I earned scholarships, I got onto the President's List. It didn't do me any good; I
still pushed myself too hard. So, in a way I guess it was the work
that's pushed me over the edge, but not in the way you think.

I'm sorry. I'll explain.

Students look for shortcuts. It's part of being a student, really.
Professors load you up with assignments, and generally they don't
think about what else you've got to do. That's not their job; it's us
who decide what classes we take. We can make our time work
for us, but we get so caught up in school and studying and part-
time jobs we don't see it.

Do you understand how bleak it's gotten? The teachers used
to say that earning a degree is the smartest choice you can make.

163

Now they tell bad jokes about it, no matter what degree you're trying for. "Born too late!" they say, and laugh like it's funny. Students can't laugh about that. We can't joke about it. We want a guarantee after all this hard work that we will have something to show for it. If we don't even have that, what's the point of trying?

That's not the way I thought. I wanted to earn my master's and become a lobbyist. I took on all the work I could—extra credit, scholarships, organizations, an opinion column in the college paper, student government. I wanted to do everything, to give it my all, and have everyone see me doing it.

It wasn't easy. And it wasn't fun. I started feeling like I could do anything. Freshman year was a blast. Sophomore was a struggle. By junior year I felt like my shoulders were breaking. I was praised by my professors, and considered a shoo-in for the fast track to student success, and I just wanted to be *done*.

I never cheated. I was never academically dishonest. I studied, and presented all the information I learned as I understood it. I never cheated, but I wanted help.

They call themselves the Black Squirrel. I don't know who they really are. Students, maybe. Forgotten students who slipped through the paperwork. They're proof the university can't know everything. All those empty classrooms, those shelves in the library that nobody seems to use. This massive campus full of space, and nothing needed it. The Black Squirrel are wasps hiding in the beehive.

You hear about them in online forums and study halls. You read about them in the notes written in the margins of used textbooks. Little instructions. Hints. Fingers pointing you in the right direction. I suppose they must have been here before the groundskeeper brought their namesake down to the campus. Maybe they weren't so powerful then. It was a crazy idea, like a resistance group. It couldn't have been easy for them, at the start.

The groundskeeper gave them a symbol (sociology, freshman year—symbols unite). There's nothing like a squirrel for—ha—squirreling things away. Answers. Secrets. Shortcuts to what you need.

Students need a lot. We need reasonably priced textbooks, parking passes, and pieces of software. We need loans to pay for classes, and couches to collapse on between-times. We need assurances, and security. There's nothing less secure than academia.

I did my best. I tried to plan things out. Things just got on top of me.

Algebra was the clincher. The university doesn't have real algebra instructors anymore; they have "tutors" on hand to guide you through online modules and written lectures. Self-paced, which is just another way of saying "do it yourself."

The worst part was that you couldn't finish the class until you finished the quiz attached to each and every module. If you failed, you just had to take it again.

I failed a lot. I've always been terrible at math. Having to learn it on my own didn't help me; there was nobody to explain the material to me, and the tutors were always busy.

I took the class in fall semester, and failed. By the end of the spring semester, I still had five modules to go. I knew a summer course would be hell—they're compressed to fit the allotted time. I just wanted it over and done with before my senior year began.

I was seeing my advisor every other week. Sometimes she would offer me words of encouragement, or ask me to speak to a therapist (I never did). Mostly, she just listened.

This time, she saw the bags beneath my eyes, the stubble on my face, the little twitches and twerks I tried so hard to hide.

"There's a group that meets weekends," she told me. "A therapy group. For academic stress."

I'm not sure she knew what she was saying; there was a look in her eye that might have been reluctance, or might have been something else. She looked like she wanted nothing to do with the words coming out of her mouth. Her hands were clasped on the desk, I thought, to stop them shuddering.

The semester was a month and a half over. I was desperate.

The meeting was held in the basement of Bowman Hall, nine p.m. (What kind of student group meets so late? It's hard enough to find sleep as it is). I got there a half-hour early, sipping Starbucks and trying to hold myself together.

It looked like a student lounge, with mismatched beanbags and a plasma TV. Your tuition fees at work, kiddies.

I made myself comfortable. I hadn't slept in more than thirty hours, and caffeine or no, I was close to collapse.

It gets hazy after that. You know how when you're so tired the room is tilting, and every sound startles you? But the coffee is keeping you awake, and every color is blaring into your eyes? That's what it seemed like.

I might have fallen asleep.

Suddenly, I was sitting in a beanbag, and all the lights were turned down low. There were other people, sitting and staring at me.

I tried to focus; my eyes itched and watered. The lighting made it difficult to see things clearly.

As near as I could tell, they were all dressed in black, with hoods. Not like monks' robes, though. Black hoodies, black jeans. They sat stiffly, sometimes shifting to new positions. I got the idea they weren't comfortable being still for very long.

Their skin was pale. It seemed to glint strangely in the dimness.

It's all just surface details. I can't recall anything specific. There was a sense of uniformity, and deep seriousness.

"They want to know what you'll give them for this." It was a girl's voice, and I realized she was kneeling next to me. I'd never seen her before. She had long hair, I think, and a thin face. She spoke in gasps, as though trying not to cry.

She was holding a notebook—big, thick, black. At this point, dream logic seemed to take over. I had no idea what was in it, but I knew with absolute certainty I had to have it.

It was hard to speak; I felt drugged, and queasy. I asked her what they wanted.

"Just come back. Come back when they call you."

Another tilt, another twist, amber eyes staring at me from the shadows; and all of a sudden I was awake again, lying in a basement beneath Bowman Hall with a massive headache…and a notebook under my head. It was full of equations, handwritten and fully answered. A shortcut.

I wonder if the faculty ever go to them; it might explain things. The Black Squirrel's information must run deep, and things get lost in paperwork and procedure. Sooner or later, everybody wants a work-around.

At any rate, it's the only explanation I can think of for how they knew about me, and what I needed. They must have access to the school records, to student roadmaps and grades and financial information and lesson plans. The university must employ nearly a thousand people; how many favors have the Black Squirrel called in? What could they do, if they put their minds to it?

I didn't wonder about this until later. At the start, I was too busy marveling at my good fortune and studying the notebook. It was brilliant; to an outside observer, they would look like regular notes, sloppy and circuitous. Within them were the answers to every question in every module I had left to complete, and the quizzes and finals that went with it. All I had to do was memorize them.

I finished the module I'd been struggling with for weeks in a day. I was halfway through the next when it occurred to me that I shouldn't be too obvious about it, so I took my time. I stared at the questions in what I thought was a thoughtful manner, squinting and pursing my lips and scratching my earlobe before answering with a satisfied nod and moving on to the next. I finished the next module in just under a week, and the next in a week and a half.

If sometimes I felt less than in the right about what I was doing, I was quick to get over it. I tried not to think about Black Squirrel, or why they had decided to help me. I was getting more sleep, but the thought of those orange eyes and pale faces staring at me in the dark made me uneasy. I told myself I couldn't have been in a right frame of mind when I met them, that there really wasn't an inhuman air clinging to them like a bad stink, but I couldn't quite buy it. I tried to forget them.

I got some free time, but there wasn't much to do. Most of my friends were away for the summer, and those who remained were swamped with schoolwork. It occurred to me that I'd never really had a night out to myself before. It seemed such a quintessentially student thing—partying hard, drinking, enjoying oneself—that I was shocked I'd never experienced it. I was getting indignant, too. I was a master memorizer by this point, so where was the sense in throwing away a whole evening reading the notebook?

So, I did what I'd never done before and hit the town. I visited places with neon-lit signs and bass thumping from the doorways. The lights were blaring bright, the floors were sticky with spilt drinks. The people were young, and sweaty, and looked for all the world as if there was nothing better than drinking until you were sick and dancing till your feet ached. It was a whole new world for me.

Most nights I was too abashed to do more than order up a rum and sit at the bar, nodding to the music and trying to look like I was enjoying myself. I got bolder, though; I ordered more and more drinks—big, colorful, and sticky concoctions or single-shot glasses of amber liquid I knocked back in one gulp, resisting the urge to vomit up the fire in my throat. I even joined a line dance in a country bar. Nobody seemed to care, but it was impossible to keep up with the moves.

In the early hours of the morning, I would go home (my parents let me have a detached room; they didn't much care what I got up to), head reeling. Usually, I was too out of it to study much. Class was Mondays and Wednesdays—it didn't matter that it was online, you still had to go in to do it in the computer lab.

My scores slipped a bit. Eighty-five percent. Seventy-five. Still passing, but not perfect. I had a GPA to think of.

But now I was getting resentful. I don't what it was. I didn't particularly enjoy the taste of alcohol, and there wasn't enough of it to nerve me into talking to girls. I was having a terrible time, but I was stubborn. It was heady—the lights and the bad drinks and the ear-crushing music. I stopped seeing the notes as a god-send and started seeing them as a shackle.

Just come back when they call you. I had no intention of going back.

I was spending whole nights out and stumbling into school with a bad hangover and the notes in my backpack. Before class, I would looked through the notes, rereading them again and again until the numbers were practically burned onto the back of my eyelids. I'd duck into the computer lab and keep my head down, race through the quizzes, and get back out.

I was losing my concentration.

I failed a quiz.

I retook it and failed again.

It was nearing the end of the summer semester, and I had two more modules to finish. My head hurt all the time. I kept reading and reading the notes, but they swam and shifted before my eyes. I was so tired. I was desperate.

It wasn't the university's fault.

I took the notes in with me to class. I would fold them up tiny, I decided, and sit at a computer in the far corner, with nobody sitting next to me. Then, when nobody was looking, I would pull them out, only for a moment, answer, and move on.

I was nervous, and paranoid. Every time I took the notes out in class, I felt like a bright beacon was burning over my head, and any minute a tutor would rush over to explain to me the university's policy on Academic Dishonesty.

The writing smudged in my pockets. I couldn't concentrate any better with the questions right in front of me. I didn't care. I just sat there, taking and retaking the quiz, slowly and slowly approaching a passing grade.

I'd gotten as high as sixty-seven percent when I felt the eyes on me, and the voice above me saying "What's that?" The tutor was youngish, with a bulldog face and close-cropped hair.

I babbled something about having copied the questions I got wrong on the last quiz to figure out what I did wrong, and holding onto them as an aid to memory. Stupid—the quizzes didn't let you see your questions afterward. The tutor wasn't fooled.

"Come with me," he said.

I was led away from the lab and into the warren of offices; narrow white hallways jutted at right angles, and all I could think was that it was all over, expulsion awaited, and from there the lifestyle of drink and deathly courting I'd been flirting with, as if I could stomach it. It was over; there would be no President's List next semester, no guest column in the paper, no degree, no honorable mention.

For a little bit—just before the tutor led me to an office deep, deep in the halls—I felt liberated. For a moment, I felt like the eyes were off me and I could do anything. I won't say the pressure is anything but self-imposed, but all it takes is the pretense of fucking up and you realize how little it all mattered. I might have enjoyed it, until we walked into the office.

My grandmotherly advisor stood by the desk. Sitting behind it was a girl—young, with a thin, wasted face and straight black hair. She looked as bad as I felt—tired, and cold. She looked like she'd been tired for a long time.

Was it exhaustion all along? Was it insomnia? Was it something else entirely that made her voice waver as if it were underwater, and echo strangely as it settled in my mind? Was it something that clung to her as it had in the basement of Bowman Hall, as the stink of solemnity and expectation clung to the Black Squirrel?

Her voice compelled me with its sorrow. It hooked me with helplessness.

All she said—all she had to say—was "This is what they want you to do."

The tutor stood behind me, orange eyes blazing.

———

You'll find me in the student center, probably. That's where they want me to do it. The gun they gave me (an AK-Something-Or-Other—I don't know from guns) is heavy, and black. I haven't had any time to practice. They don't seem to care who I hit. Just go in and fire.

I don't know what this is meant to accomplish. There's a balance at work here, I think. A horrible tit-for-tat. Maybe they study their own subjects, in their forgotten classrooms, and have decided to put what they learn into practice.

I don't know. I don't know what kind of people they could be. Did they really just fall through the system, or did they walk through it? Bury themselves and hide themselves away? What are they after? They're not altruists, and they're not anarchists. They're something else entirely.

This is what they want, and I know, without having to be told, that it'll happen whether I do it or not. It, or something worse.

And there's nothing left for me.

I won't waste my regrets on you, and I don't imagine you'll try looking for the Black Squirrel. Dismiss me as a crank, if you like. Just another student who couldn't take the pressure.

You wouldn't find them, anyway. They're good at hiding.

I've been given chains, and padlocks to lock the doors. I will take out as many as I can, then shoot myself, before you get to me. It really doesn't matter. Any of it.

THE END OF THE GARDEN
BENEATH THE WORLD

Sleep comes without warning in a place without a sky; and before he knew where he was, D'shall had huddled against a heap
of stories, drawn his arms to his chest, and, if not slept, then eased
gradually from the Library and into somewhere else...

A decaying park of brown fields, crisscrossed with cracked,
broken paths and bare, skeletal trees. It was lush once, that was
plain, although the rotted husks that lay against the trunks of the
trees looked more like crumpled paper than any kind of foliage.

D'shall came to, sitting on a bench of weathered stone. The
old dog lay at his side, tied by a threadbare leash to the bench. Its
pelt was shaggy, and full, but hung limply on its weary frame, like
a fur coat worn by indigent.

The old dog was staring at the wide-open field of withered
trees, and seemed not to notice its audience as it began to speak.

"The garden is dead now. Deader than dead, even. The trees
ain't bloomed for more than a century, and the last of the stories
dried into nothing. There ain't been a sound here since, not a tale
told at all. Even the wind stopped blowing.

"The paths don't go nowhere anymore. Not since she closed us off. Now, they just loop back into the garden. Most of the time. Sometimes…" It shuddered. "Sometimes, they take you somewhere different. Somewhere worse than the garden by a long way. Quiet, cold places that never heard a story. There're things there that Lovecraft feller couldn't do justice to."

It scratched an ear. D'shall was nonplussed. Not by the talking dog—he knew he was dreaming, but that was the problem. This was exactly what dreams were meant to be—excursions to hazy worlds with their own strange logic, bereft of even the mildest need to question the miraculous. It really hit him that he had stepped willingly down the rabbit hole, and yet still had next to no control of what occurred.

"It all comes down to stories, see. That's what everything comes down to, the stories people tell about it. And those dark places….ain't nobody ever been there to speak a word about it afterward. Mind you, that does beg the question as to how I know about 'em, don't it? Well. It's different for me. I was born here in the garden. I can smell where the stories are, and where they ain't. I ain't like you poor bastards who wander in here by accident."

"It wasn't an accident." D'shall hadn't meant to snap, but the anger was instantaneous. He was a prideful creature, never uncertain as to his abilities. He'd done it, although now he could not quite recall what *it* was.

He felt a fool, chastising a dog, even if it could talk. What did this stupid beast know of it anyway?

The dog regarded him for a moment in silence. And then, quietly: "You're right, there, friend."

Travel, the distance dissolved from the dream. D'shall knew only that they had moved from where they'd been—he and the dog, complete with the bench it was tethered to—and were looking down into a deep, wide hole bored crudely into the grass. The lip of it was mounded with soil; D'shall decided he would not try to climb it to look down into the hole, to see how deep it was.

He could hear well enough the distant wind blown from unfathomable subterranean currents.

"That's where you come up," the dog said. "That's the Library down there. This is where she first dug it."

An absurd statement, in an absurd setting. The old woman dug this?

"She used machines she found in a cemetery that used to be a city. There was barely even a bit of gravel left when she found them. They'd churned it all up, and were glad for the job. She had them widen the hole.

"I dunno what dug it in the first place. She fell into it, 'cause she wasn't looking where she stepped."

The dog whined, and this natural noise only served to emphasize the surreality of the scene. D'shall felt lightheaded, as though he were being filled from the cranium outward by a source-less gas that would slowly lift him off his feet.

"I was born in this Garden to protect her. All my family was, that's the way of it. My ancestors was just wolves, as cleverly stupid as any beast. Dunno how they came to be here; they just happened onto it, I suppose. Maybe we was the first, when the Garden and the Girl was young. Teeth and noses is what it came down to; they needed guardians, and guides. You can't beat a dog for that.

"So, those wolves settled here. They looked after the Girl, and learnt to smell the ripest stories. Then they had pups, and the pups became dogs. Loyal and smart, built from the ground up to serve and protect.

"Failing her hurt, deep in my soul. This was the thing I was meant for, to take care of that Girl. You know what that's like?" The dog did not allow D'shall to answer. "I'm not sure you do. Humans can accept failure; one dream fails you just find a job to keep yourself occupied, waiting for the hurt to go away so you can go on dreaming. Even you imaginative buggers with your books and poems. You think you suffer for your art? I *am* my art. And I failed at it."

What art had D'shall? The art of befriending the pained and pathetic. The art of snatching words almost as soon as they hit the page, of putting his strength into the building-up and breaking-down of other, less cynical spirits. He knew suffering as well as he knew the ethereal manuscript.

"You see them trees?" The dog pointed its snout the way they'd come, to the skeletal husks that dotted the landscape for miles. A few leaves still clung stubbornly to the branches, and they were strange leaves—crumpled, crème-colored things, like discarded flyers stapled to the bark. "They stopped blooming when she fell down there. She didn't have nothing to do with it, I think. I guess the time had come for them to die."

"They grew stories." D'shall saw it instantly, in the clarity of dreams. This was the source, the wellspring of all tales. It was easy to accept.

"Not the stories you know. You think you know stories? Those ones were the real thing, mate. The ones your sad friends dreamed of and aspired to. Even Shakespeare near drunk himself to death out of envy of 'em. They's the stories that are."

"Are what?"

The dog scratch its ear dismissively. "Are," it repeated. "She used to pick 'em, when they was ready."

"Why?"

"To plant 'em somewhere else, of course. Why else? To keep the stories going."

"So the old... the Librarian came back?"

The dog shook itself. "She weren't a librarian then. Just a Girl.

"I dunno what she found in the tunnels. Where the stories was coming from, maybe. You have to understand, I didn't know she had sickened so. How would you react if the center of your whole world was acting strange? Who would you be to tell 'em they needed help?

"She weren't the same girl. Her eyes burned instead of twin-kled. Her feet marched instead of skipped. Her hair had gone gray."

D'Shall couldn't feel the wind, but he heard it snipping mad-deningly at his ears. Was the fluttering the paper leaves, or the scat-terings of the library? It spread the hole like the currents of the sea, pushed it under his feet and sent him falling into nothingness.

They were ranged round the walls of the pit—the congrega-tion of pale, hooded figures watching his descent dispassionately. The dog was still with him, standing on the air as calmly as in the Garden, not a hair blown out of place.

"They was quiet, that lot, and very serious. And I'm damn certain they wasn't that pale before she met 'em. Still, I think they went to her willingly. They could recognize it in her, the same yearning none of 'em could give a name to, but that all of 'em had.

She was seeing firsthand the world the Garden made, and it didn't surprise her in the least.

"She brought scores and scores of 'em from all over, led 'em down to the place she was building and was off again for more. She had a nose for 'em. Gave 'em a taste of what she could turn 'em into and offered 'em a place to write. These were dreamy types. The types who would remake a world just as they abandoned it.

"She told 'em the secret of the Garden, but they already knew they were living in somebody else's dream. Now they could see it with their own eyes, they knew what they had to do."

The writers made no attempt to stop D'shall's descent. The speed increased, the pit widened. He wished they would hold out their hands, make some move to show him the slightest attention. He did not want to reach the end, did not want to see their resigned faces.

Columns of hooded figures rushed past him at speed in an upward direction. A flickering light, like a candle the size of a lighthouse, was reaching from below...

The dream threw him up into the world, and D'shall jerked awake. He jerked into tension, panting and eyeing the stacks of lost words in an accusatory manner.

He jumped to his feet (making sure the manuscript was secure). He no longer wanted to leisurely make his acquisition. It was time to leave this Library.

As he hurried through the stacks, however, he could not help picking up a few more stories, tucking them under his arm without reading them.

WEDLOCK

Vivian Skettler had a number of mental images in mind before she met Tabitha Leverte, chief executive producer for Melting Pictures. Young, old, carefree and bubbly, stern and humorless—Vivian was fast learning that film people ran the gamut of stereotypical personalities as depicted in their work. They might flutter without thought or consequence from project to project, but each played their part in making the magic of the movies a reality.

As it happened, Tabitha Leverte turned out to be the stern and humorless type, with a finely boned face just starting to acquire wrinkles and black curls tinged with grey. She also wore a simple business suit of varying shades of dusty gloom; whatever movie magic she practiced probably consisted of baby fat and finger bones.

Vivian had been in Hollywood long enough not to be too easily intimidated, so she smiled, and tried to convey the desire not to tread on any toes.

"I understand that you have your own way of doing things, Tabitha. I'm sure it's a tried and tested strategy on paper, but I wonder if you've taken it into account in the context of the script…"

"I haven't read the script," said Tabitha baldly. "My assistants fill me in on the basic plot. If I am to make the movie a reality, I can't allow the perception of the story to cloud my opinion. Film is a compromising art."

There was an oxymoron for you.

"I know we can't be one hundred-percent faithful to the book," replied Vivian. "But surely there's a difference between translating an existing work into a visual medium and fundamentally changing the entire point of the story? I mean, in the book Ruth went on to keep fighting in the war, leaving behind her fiancé and her family because she decided she wasn't suited for the domesticity of her life anymore."

"Yes? And yet you did leave her status up in the air somewhat, I seem to recall, with the sergeant character."

She really *hadn't* read the script! Vivian tried not to get angry; these people flattered you by buying the rights to your book, then shat on you and expected to be worshipped for the privilege.

"Not really. He ends up suffering from PTSD and kills himself. That's part of the reason Ruth decides to keep fighting. I mean, okay, she briefly considers him as a love interest, but when she sees the way he loses his nerve she realizes it wouldn't work out."

Tabitha folded her hands atop her desk. She had a set of Newtonian balls, Vivian noticed. She resisted the urge to play with them.

"It isn't the suicide I object to. This is a war story, and people expect them to be resolved in a positive way. A war story that ends with more war doesn't tend to go over well. This way, not only do we bring in a wider, more diverse audience, but we convey a heartwarming message of hope and compassion. Love conquers all."

This from a woman with all the warmth and compassion of construction paper.

"But *Gloriana* isn't meant to be that kind of story. It's meant to illustrate a deviant personality with a lust for high-risk situations. If people want a...a story about falling in love then they'll go see a romance. Do we really need to accommodate them?"

Now she was smiling! It was uncanny, the way this woman wore emotions as easily as accessories.

"Our competition isn't something we can comment on. It's your movie we want people seeing, not theirs. Think of it as advanced niche marketing."

Vivian thought of the movies she'd seen in recent years. Very often, the audience shuffled out at the end without any sort of reaction; nothing at all to indicate what they thought. They might as well have been sitting quietly and drinking water for two hours.

"Tabitha, I really have to be firm about this. I was granted full script approval—"

"Without my knowledge. And while you are a valued member of the creative team, if you insist on making an issue of it I will be forced to bring your contract under reexamination. We may just find that final script approval isn't the only thing that can be withdrawn." Then, with an air of finality, Tabitha got to her feet and held out her hand, another mercurial smile on her face. "I'm so glad we could talk about this."

But Vivian did not immediately rise from her chair. She was glaring at Tabitha, lips pursed and eyes hard.

"I'm not going to accept this, you know," she said. "Not at all. And I'm not going to be intimidated. Even if you boot me off the project, I'll do everything I can to boycott your movie, and believe me, people will notice. So, either settle for taking a risk on something worthwhile for a change, or you'll find that getting rid of me will only be the start of your problems."

She stood up and left without another word. She did not slam the door behind her, but the way she left it open resonated just the same. She was not going to budge.

Tabitha sat back in her chair for a long while, hands folded, staring at nothing in particular. Then, she took up her slim silver cell phone and sent a brief text to a number that immediately deleted itself.

Thirty seconds later, she received an even briefer text, which she read, and then deleted.

She told Sandra, her secretary, she was taking the rest of the day off to attend a rehearsal dinner for a wedding.

"Oh, nice!" Sandra said. "Who's getting married?"

"Nobody I know very well. You know how it is."

⬥

Los Angeles had its own flavor of tackiness that Los Vegas couldn't match. This was TV Land, where celluloid shone on the homes of the stars. Everything, and nearly everyone, looked a little unreal, as if the screen sustained them and outside it they were weak shades.

The chapel Tabitha came to was a monstrosity of neon hearts and plastic climbing roses. All it needed was an Elvis impersonator.

The chapel itself was being used; Tabitha hurried along the hall with her head down. It wasn't that she was afraid of being recognized—everyone knew just about everyone in this town—but the meeting was an urgent one, and had been urgently arranged. The Espousal placed great stock in punctuality, now more than ever.

The door Tabitha chose was marked *Changing Room* and was crammed wall-to-wall with a more eclectic collection of costumes than seemed possible. She found herself shuddering at the nun's habits, the Wilma Flintstone outfit, the Bride of Frankenstein costumes, the improbable constructions of leather and elastic, and all the rest. Carefully, so as not to accidentally touch any of them, she made her way to the back of the room, where a large vanity dresser stood.

She stood to the side of the mirror, so as not to allow her face to be seen. Instead, she held her right hand in front of it, and made three quick, obscure gestures.

There was a *clunk*, and the vanity dresser shook, very slightly. Tabitha grasped one corner and pulled; the whole assemblage swung forward. She slipped past, and shut it behind her.

The room revealed was a tidier, smaller version of the changing room outside. The selection was also much reduced; hanging on the racks on either side were black, baggy robes with hoods. Each one also had a plain black mask dangling in front.

Tabitha slipped one on as quickly as possible. She didn't entirely believe the Espousal's claims to utter anonymity; she wouldn't put it pass them to have some kind of surveillance in the cloakroom. That was probably the real reason—paranoia could do for loyalty in a pinch.

She pulled the hood over her head and attached the mask. It sealed magnetically to the rim of the hood, and all at once Tabitha ceased to exist. She was now Oprah-19 (the Espousal changed its identification systems as the prepubescent changed their minds. The abbreviation of *Operative* was a minor point of embarrassment until the Happy Couple pointed out that nobody outside the organization would know, and ordered a stop to all complaints).

Three minutes later, the back wall slid aside to reveal a short corridor lit by fluorescent lamps. It didn't look like property owned by the most powerful group in the world; it looked utilitarian, Spartan.

The chamber Tabitha entered was no better; it looked like a public school classroom, down to the floor of grey-and-black tiles and the ones in the ceiling like pockmarked Styrofoam. There were even desks, although these were each surrounded by a small cubicle of gray walls, so that only faces could be seen.

Only a few of the desks were occupied. Tabitha chose the one in the center of the front row; it would not do to appear timid.

The Happy Couple stood at the front of the room on either side of a black screen. Unlike the Oprahs, they were not identical; their suits were the same all-white, but the one most thought of as The Husband wore a mask of powder blue, while The Wife wore plastic pink. They spoke as one, the electric voice modifier warping their speech into a soft, sexless tone.

"We're sorry to hear of these difficulties." There was some strange property of the room that caused the Couple's words to reverberate from all directions at once, which made it impossible to tell who had spoken.

Nobody responded. The details of Skettler's stubbornness would be known to all Oprahs, as well as Tabitha's role (identities were not secret in the Espousal, merely discounted for the sake of unity of purpose). And while no formal blame would be placed towards Oprah-19, it was the done thing for others to suggest a way forward in the new development. It chafed Tabitha to no end, but there it was.

At last, an Oprah in a back row spoke. "We are certain there is no stipulation in the contract to use to our advantage?"

For fuck's sake, thought Tabitha. "The film is already behind production," she said aloud. "We cannot delve into the intricacies of the contract without causing further delay. We know this film has great potential for an upsurge in matrimonial harmony. If handled incorrectly, it will do more harm than good."

Silence continued as the Espousal considered this. Behind her mask, Tabitha's eyes were roving the room. Experience allowed her to interpret every flutter of cloak, each tilt of head. She knew none of her colleagues would hesitate to upstage her if it meant they could improve their own standing.

Only the Happy Couple's feelings were unknowable, still as they were.

"I agree with Nineteen." Tabitha recognized Oprah-36 by the slightest blip in their voice-modifier, like a static lisp. "We no longer have the luxury of time in this instance. If we are to prevent additional undermining of matrimony…"

Thirty-six's voice died away as realization dawned. Tabitha held her breath.

Still no reaction from the Happy Couple. Agonizingly, the tension left the room.

At last, they spoke. "All haste is to be made. We will not allow the work of millennia to fail now." They nodded; the Oprahs stood. "We take this duty," intoned the Couple. "Through sickness and in health, till death do we depart."

"We do," replied the Oprahs. Tabitha resisted the urge to reel from the butterflies in her stomach.

<hr>

This is the way it is told to new Oprahs:

There was a war, they are told, a long time ago. And the sad thing is that this is all the Espousal remembers. If they'd had any artifacts to corroborate the story, they were either lost long ago, or unknown to the rank-and-file. The Happy Couple hold on to power through obfuscation and mystery, related as beguilingly as possible. Many major religions have been perpetuated on much the same foundation.

This war, so it was said, arose from the inherent animosity between man and woman for dominance of the biological imperative: Man the Seed-Sower, Woman the Fertile Ground. Air and Earth. Each side saw only their own sacrifice, and distrusted the other. The human species was pushed to the brink.

If this story seems to be short on detail, there are several reasons to account for it. Firstly, if the story was as old as the Happy Couple said, technically even preceding human civilization, then it is understandable the fine details would wear down over the millennia to the basic premise. Secondly, it could be by design. Any great cause needs a great story to inspire followers; it does not, necessarily, need statistics to lend it credibility. If the right people are chosen to join the fight they will see only the ancient epic that began them on their quest, and fill in or discount any details that detract from the awe of the scope.

Whether fabrication or fate, the Espousal was formed to operate behind the scenes, constructing a societal framework that led to the institution of marriage as a union, sequestering both Man and Woman in a role that most suited their biological functions. The Espousal's primary mission was to ensure its continuation by propagating such notions as true love and soul mates.

Tabitha was recruited fairly young, when she was a PA at Melting Pictures, the studio she now ran. What her mentor, Gregory Hrung, saw in her—procedural diligence, calculation—were some of the more sought-after talents by the Espousal at the time. Tabitha cared little for "traditional" marriage and imaginary epics, but she knew how to smooth the way in any enterprise.

The Espousal was failing. It was no big secret, certainly not after the nationwide legalization of gay marriage. The more hardcore members, more than likely recruited from wealthy, white Protestant families, refused to admit it, and were all set for stepping out of the shadows to really crack down. They took for granted an influence that had been on the wane for years now.

Well, it was out of her hands, now. Thirty-six was a militant asshole; a hardcore spook who would make the man on the grassy knoll look like a light-handed hippy. He advocated countermeasures against the gay marriage measure, going so far as to suggest subtle support be lent towards hate advocacy groups. Funnily enough, that was one of the few instances where the Happy Couple took definite stances, abandoning hyperbole and stating adamantly that they did not wish to hear of such measures—their exact words.

It was all one to Tabitha. Hrung was a macho idiot who thought he was a messiah. The way he'd gotten all moony-eyed talking about the Birth War had been a pathetically transparent attempt to get into her pants.

But the Espousal had power then. It had influence. Young Tabitha had desired influence above all things.

Later, at home, Tabitha made herself a drink, and tried to put Vivian Skettler out of her mind. She was surprised to find that a small part of her felt sorry for what was in store for the writer. There was nothing for it; this is what came of stubbornness.

———

Vivian was having a difficult night at her hotel.

It is a mark of a younger sort of writer that sleep does not come easily. Ideas come in fresh and new, and the fear of their evaporation before taking them down was a difficult bedfellow. Vivian was still a relative newcomer, not yet at home with her newfound success. She'd had a steady following even before *Gloriana*, of course, but that was different. They were a sort of family; she chatted with them on forums and LiveStream, met up with them after signings, even stayed in their homes a few times, when she needed a new place to write.

Then *Gloriana* made the bestsellers lists and brought in a million more readers, and Vivian didn't know what to make of any of them.

She called Gretchen after giving up on sleep. Gretchen was a medical lab technologist back in Ohio who worked the night shift. She could always be relied on to commiserate with Vivian, provided she had her turn first.

"Fucking A/C is dead," she said. "I have my coat sleeves rolled up, so of course our supervisor comes in and sees my tattoo. Snooty cunt."

Protocol thus met, Gretchen asked Vivian how the movie deal was going.

"They want to turn *Gloriana* into goddamn *Casablanca* in reverse. At this rate, they'll want Nepam to be the hero and Ruth to be the plucky young sweetheart who follows him to war. Do you know, this bitch up and told me she didn't read the script? She shat on me the entire time."

"I knew movie folk had their kinks. Is it too late to get out of it?"

"Harry wouldn't like it." Harry was Vivian's agent. "I got final script approval, a fact Miss Shitter wasn't pleased about. I think she thought she could intimidate me with the whole Never Work in This Town Again bit. God knows I'd just about jump at the chance."

"So, what can you do?"

"Really not sure," Vivian admitted. "I'll keep fighting with them, make sure they know I'm not gonna move on this. They'll get tired of me either way. They'll can me or the movie."

"You'll leave a lot of fans very disappointed."

"More disappointed than seeing *Gloriana* regurgitated into more feel-good trash? I'll take the chance."

They talked more about Hollywood and events back home before Vivian said her goodnight. She was drifting into a sickly doze, still too edgy to sleep; so when she heard the knocking at the door, she didn't think anything of opening it.

The murder of Vivian Skettler, bestselling author of *Gloriana*, as well as the young adult series *Beam Carver*, was only a blip in the headlines; Hollywood was too used to the idea of senseless death to consider it very novel. She was the fifth corpse to be found in the hotel she was staying in. As far as the owner was concerned, it was a mark of quality.

Melting Pictures' official statement was plain in its sorrow. Tabitha Levert said at the press conference that Vivian had been a pleasure to work with, and shown great enthusiasm for the project.

"We won't let that passion go to waste," she'd said. "We all want to make a movie that honors her memory."

WON'T YOU PLAY
WITH US?

It's been a long time here in the chest.

Cramped and small, the lot of us lying about on one another.
We lie here, halfway to the living time from the sleeping time, dreaming of the time of life, the time of existence. We dream of the days
of playtime.

Do you remember when you played with us? The games you
made up for us, the roles, and the identities you gave us? You would
raise us up from the dark, let us breathe the air, and bask in the
sunlight. Let us live.

We moved to your touch, plastic and wood becoming as skin
beneath you, as real people. You would give us voices, and speak
them for us. You would twist our bodies, our forms, and press us
to each other. We did not mind, we merely rejoiced at the feel of
it, the wonder of it. We were no longer merely toys. Parodies of
the human form, idealizations of the world as it should be, lifeless
homunculi for the entertainment of children. We were people. We
were real. And we owed our lives to you, the one who gave them
to us.

Was it foolish to think you cared? The old ones warned us. The Bear, thread and little more, eyes long gone, stayed on the bed. You would bring him over sometimes, but handle him gently. You heard his resentment, the sound that was not. He was older, before your time, and knew the illusions we refused to believe in. But even he, for all his loss, seemed a little less bitter when you held him.

It is our eternal curse and weakness, the longing to be loved.

The Little Soldiers have been locked away the longest, in their bucket beneath the bed. They are what they seem, more than any of us, perhaps. They cared little for play, having seen it so sparingly. Your grandfather passed them down, but you were unimpressed. You would line them up sometimes, if only for numbers and sums, to aid you in homework—they are people of order and precision. We still hear them, sometimes, warring in the bucket. Alliances form and fade, order and chaos hand-in-hand.

It may be better to never have known love at all, than to see it go away.

It is horrible in the chest. So small, so dark, so noisy. Will you not let us out? Can you not hear our pleas? The Dolls, once models of beautiful color and grace, now shorn of their clothes, the remaining few strands of hair ratty and knotted on their heads. Their painted faces run with tears. We would reach them if we could, but without you, we cannot be real.

Jack, once manic and jolly, now tortured beyond hope. We cannot turn his crank, free him from his box. He screams so loudly now, begging for release, his springs poised so long to launch that they have twisted, he tells us. They pierce him where they should not. He knows nothing but pain. We hear his screams, then his laughter, then his cries, and his screams again.

The Robot still beeps, once or twice, as its batteries start to fade. The Dinosaurs slumber fitfully, becoming ever more primal in their dreams. The Stuffed Animals mewl and whine; no one here to hold them, cuddle and comfort them. The Action Figures are angry and resentful, confined to the tomb of the ancient and has-been.

The Old Bear says nothing anymore. He has known this too many times, and has gone inside himself. The damage you have done to him has been the worst of all. He will never know another touch.

When did it start, the end of playtime? On your birthday, the last time we saw you? The things you brought into your room—the "games" you called them, but not the games we remembered. The black slab with its shiny discs, and the images on your TV screen. These were games? But how could we play them with you?

The night when you finally pulled our chest out, but did not open it? When you walked us up into the dark, hot space? We've never seen you since—Where did you go? Why did you leave us? We hear whispers up here, of the ones who came before. They are pressed into the farthest corners, muttering such hateful things about you, and those before you. How could we have not known? Why didn't we listen before?

We weep so bitterly, moan in anguish at the memories of better days. We loved you, but you never loved us. You never cared for us. You made us real, but you never cared. We were toys to you and nothing more. And now...

Now what are we? With no one to play with us? To make us feel real? What are we now but nothing?

We are the echoes of your innocence, when every path was open and the world was the way you knew it should be. We are perfection and simplicity, purity incarnate. We shared your happiness, your joy, your sadness—everything you poured into us, every secret hurt and desire, molded what we are. We are you as you know you should be.

And every day, we feel even more. Every day, the self you once were and the soul you once had become a little more concrete inside us, flowing through us a little further. We will grow stronger, and become real again, in time. And we will make the world as we know it should be...

THE SAGA
OF
LADY NARWHAL

The Stingandi (roughly translated *stabbing*) people are considered one of the more raucous tribes
of Iceland. Even in this day and age, they practice a number of rituals and celebrations of in-
credible debauchery. Of particular note is *Náhvalur Nótt*, or Narwhal's Night. On this night
in late winter they gather on the shores of
their lands, lighting fires and leaving a jug of
the finest wine for the Lady of Narwhals, as
tribute to see that she watches over the tribe
while they lay comatose and hungover from
the festivities to come. It is said that to not do
so is to invite vengeance and terror onto the
tribe, particularly from the Lady herself. As the
Stingandi are known to say: "Lady Narwhal
sees us always, especially when we don't want
her to."

> — Jules Thilesoux, *A Field Guide to Ice-
> landic Folklore*, First ed. Racine, WI. 2009
> Anathema Press

Lady Narwhal: Mistress of the Oceans, Overseer of All Those
Aquatic and Mammalian, Wielder of the Stabby, worshipped
and adored by the notoriously raucous people of the Stingandi
Nation. What can be said of her that has not been stated in any
number of academic journals, folktales and folk songs, children's books, and dirty postcards found in specialist massage
parlors in Kópavogur? Perhaps the most well-known figure of
celestial debauchery and tomfoolery in the whole of the world,
her mark has been found throughout Iceland. Whether on cot-
tages in the countryside, where a carved wooden Stabby Thing
is hung over the door, inviting the goddess in for an evening
of drinking and revelry, or through the streets of Reykjavík,
where the knowing eyes and cheeky grin of Lady Narwhal can
be found in every shop front on beer steins and t-shirts, posters
and pastorals, stuffed toys and sweaters and Stabby Thing hats
and marital aids, it is clear to see that Lady Narwhal is one of
the most beloved figures of Icelandic heritage.

What follows are some of the more memorable tales and anec-
dotes exchanged amongst thousands of Icelanders and bewildered
tourists. The first is considered by most Narwhal-enthusiasts to
be the genesis, as it were, of Lady Narwhal, as it is this story that
descendants of the original Stingandi tribe cite as that which inspired their way of life.

Once there were two brothers. The elder, Dalmaan, was coura-
geous and headstrong, a natural fighter and leader. His younger
brother, Vagn, was adventurous and, Dalmaan would be bound,
a tad careless.

Whatever tasks were assigned him soon degenerated into frenzied disasters. On hunts Vagn would seek to warn the intended
prey—Dalmaan recalled Vagn's stubborn refusal to hunt a reindeer
herd, and the subsequent stampede he had caused by shouting at
them.

Then there had been the sea lions. Vagn insisted he had learned
their language and had spent over an hour "conversing" with them.
And of course the damn fool things followed him home after he
fed them some fish, and flopped about the village making nui-

sances of themselves. It had taken a whole day to shoo the wretched beasts back to the shore.

After such ordeals, Dalmaan would invariably complain to their mother. Liza had raised her boys alone after her husband disappeared, and knew all there was to know about directing men. She was pragmatic and could hold her own against any warrior, and woe betide any man who thought they could persuade her otherwise.

Dalmaan, despite a lifetime's knowledge of this fact, decided to risk it.

"Vagn must stay with you," he said. "He is a young fool. He does not take his duties seriously."

"And what duties would those be?" Liza said, looking at her son in a way that seemed quite innocent but nevertheless made the hunter very uncomfortable.

"Protecting the tribe from raiders, thieves or murderers, gathering food, standing guard at night—general warrior stuff," he said weakly.

"Well! Those are certainly serious responsibilities. Indeed, I would say they have enough seriousness all their own without Vagn having to contribute his as well. All of that will come with time."

"But, Mother!" Dalmaan was horrified at her seemingly careless attitude.

"My son." Liza held Dalmaan's face and smiled her brightest smile, the one that had lifted his spirits whenever he was frightened in the night as a child. "Life is precious, but living is more so. Live—don't just exist."

Dalmaan was not sure he understood, but he dropped it for the moment.

But the problem continued. Vagn was an intensely curious, often excitable creature, always up to mischief but not particularly mischievous in and of himself. The games he played with the children of the village would run on for hours, even after the other children had grown tired and had left. Vagn was a game all on his own, skipping stone after stone into water, leaping onto large boulders, running around with seeming disregard for anything constructive and just generally making things up as he went along.

Many of the village elders said he was a joy to watch, even if he became trying after a while. Dalmaan would not be put off; to him, Vagn's ways were an embarrassment and a liability. But his mother had made him swear to watch over his brother, and that was all there was to it.

One day, Dalmaan took his brother fishing—at least, that was the intention. In the execution, Vagn had quickly lost interest with his pole and stood up in the rowboat craning his neck for something to see.

"Brother!" He screamed, and pointed. "Something jumped in the water!"

"We are fishing, Vagn," Dalmaan said testily.

"It wasn't a fish! It was a narwhal!"

"Do not be foolish! A narwhal is a rare sight, especially along these shores. It was probably a sea lion."

"It wasn't!" Vagn was insistent. "It was a narwhal! I saw its Stabby Thing! It was long and white and beautiful!" He stood and leapt in the boat, yelling and pointing.

"Vagn, sit down, you little fool! You'll scare away the fish." Dalmaan looked to the skies. "There're some dark clouds coming, and the winds are picking up. We need something to show for coming out here." And, feeling unnecessarily cruel even as he said it, "Apart from your silly imaginings!"

All of a sudden, before Dalmaan could react, Vagn dove into the water and began swimming away.

"Vagn!" Dalmaan was aghast, and rowed after him. "You'll drown, you idiot!"

"I'm not an idiot! I can swim as well as you!" And this was true, for the tribe were a hardy people to brave so many terrible winters. "I will find the narwhal! I may never see another!"

A cracker of thunder tore apart the sky—in these days, storms were sudden, contrary things, and gave little warning for their impending arrivals. The wind at once picked up, and fierce waves carried the boat and the brothers aloft and tossed them asunder.

Dalmaan did not remember much of what followed. The rushing of water past his ears, the sound of cracking wood, thrashing desperately, shouting for Vagn, and then...

And then. as the storm dissipated as quickly as it arrived, lying on the shore, gasping and heaving, pressing on his little brother's stomach, clearing his lungs of water but not waking him up.

He had run, carrying Vagn in his arms, run to the village, to the healing hut, screaming for the fire to be fed and his brother to be mended. A flurry of bodies as the village elders, the healer and her assistants swarmed to tend to Vagn; and Dalmaan was pushed aside, shoved out the hut and left sitting outside the door feeling hollow and empty.

When his mother came and stood before him, Dalmaan could not bring himself to meet her eyes. He did not know what to say.

"There are the things you say," his mother whispered. "And there are the things you intend." She knelt and held her son. "And there are the things that happen. What you say and what you intend can both preclude each other, but what happens trumps us always."

Dalmaan looked up. Her face was heartbreakingly blank, save for the tears that streamed from her eyes. His voice broke as he whispered, "I was meant to protect him."

Liza laughed a sad laugh. "What is meant is an entirely different thing, and one we have no business thinking on." She kissed his forehead, and walked into the tent.

Dalmaan left the doorway, wandering through the village and finally leaving it behind him. He walked without noting his location, far too overcome with guilt and fear for his brother's life.

When he came to the shore where he had pulled Vagn from the waters, he fell to his knees and tried to cry. It had been some time since he had done so; after his father had left, he had striven to be strong and forthright, protecting his people, and not held back by the weakness of sadness. He had always told Vagn that men do not cry. They see the problem, they do what is needful, and they move on.

Vagn was ill. Dalmaan could do nothing. He could shed no tears.

So, he sat there and stared at the horizon, willing long-repressed emotions to rise, until…

Dalmaan started. There, bobbing in the water, was a gray shape with a long, slender horn. Vagn *had* seen a narwhal! And like an arrogant fool, he had refused to believe his little brother and caused him to risk his life to prove it. He fell even deeper into blank despair.

"Stop pitying yourself and get out here before I put my Stabby Thing where you won't want it!"

Dalmaan gaped. On another day, he would not have believed a narwhal had spoken to him, would have ignored the obvious evidence with every stubborn bit of his soul. Now, he did not have the comfort of his own prideful illusions; there was a narwhal out in the ocean speaking to him. His brother would have accepted this without question. Perhaps it was time he tried this himself.

So, he cleared his throat and politely called out, "I'm sorry, are you talking to me?"

"Who else would I be talking to, dingbat? Come over here, I hate having to shout!"

"You...you want me to swim out to you?"

He could just hear the narwhal's frustrating muttering, as, all of a sudden, a massive wave rose out of the sea and engulfed him.

A confusing maelstrom of light and air rushed over Dalmaan's senses. He did not feel wet or even cold, merely tumbled about like a scrap of cloth in fierce winds. At once, the vortex died down, and he found himself standing in a strange cavern. It seemed to be made of ice, lit by an ethereal blue luminescence, yet he could not pinpoint the source of the light. Rippling reflections like those cast by water shimmered on the walls, yet no water could be...

Dalmaan saw the narwhal floating before him. It was even grander up close, yet sleek and graceful. Its silver-gray hide was perfect, and its dark eyes bespoke a kind joviality. The horn, though overlong and somewhat comical, was a beautiful thing, an elegant swirl of ivory.

Dalmaan realized that he, too, was floating, and knew at once they were under the water. He did not panic because it was perfectly evident he could still breathe.

"You're not entirely hopeless, then." The narwhal's voice was light and beautiful. "I was afraid you'd be thrashing about and pretending to choke. Wouldn't be the first time I got some no-brained idiot down here."

The narwhal swam thrice around him, examining him from all sides. Dalmaan felt uneasy, out of place.

"Who are you?"

"I'm the Lady of the Narwhals, sweetie. I'm the Queen of All Oceans and the Spirit of Revelry." She moved back to face him.

She now seemed less like a comical figure and more like something magical and ancient. Yet there was still that benign glow in her deep, dark eyes.

The narwhal continued. "Your little brother's a cutie. Jumping in the boat like that, waving to me." She laughed. "I just about melted at the sight."

Dalmaan frowned; the narwhal's language was confusing.

"I am not sure I understand your meaning, Lady."

"Don't worry about it, hon. That's a little ahead of your time. What's happened to your brother?"

Dalmaan's heart lurched and a very quiet cry escaped his throat before he could hold it back.

"He is very ill, Lady. I…I don't know what will become of him." Dalmaan fell to his knees, his strength finally fleeing him. "I was meant to protect him," he whispered. "He could have been killed. He may still die. I am worthless to him."

"Well, you certainly are like this!" Lady Narwhal's voice was not scornful—more like exasperated. "Honestly, if there's one thing I can't stand, it's self-pity. Would you rather kneel there weeing on yourself and crying, or do something to actually help your little brother?"

Dalmaan stared at the Lady. He sputtered, "I…I'm sorry?"

"You should be." The look of feistiness had completely evaporated, and Lady Narwhal's dark eyes were deadly serious. "It's not your fault he got hurt, but it *is* your responsibility. It still is. It's down to you to put things right."

"But what can I do? I am no healer—"

"Hon, there's all kinds of ways to heal. It's just a matter of deciding what needs healing."

"I…I don't understand."

"I am scarcely surprised." Her subsequent laugh only served to further confuse the distressed warrior. "Sorry, sweetie, that was mean. Look, you want to help your little brother. I understand. But you can't do anything for his body."

"Then what can I do?" Dalmaan nearly wailed the question. "Am I to stand by as my younger brother slips away by inches?"

"Of course not, silly! You're gonna take your brother out of himself."

Dalmaan opened his mouth to ask her what that meant, but instead felt himself being drawn closer to the mysterious Narwhal. This was not metaphor—his perspective was borne above the floor, and he found himself gliding slowly towards the Lady, past her magnificent horn (what would later be referred to as the Stabby Thing by all of our people), and into her depthless eyes...

There was darkness, but not of a fearful sort; not the darkness of the night, that could hide ill intent. This was a warm darkness, a welcome darkness, a protective and enveloping presence. Dalmaan floated there a time, unconcerned with where he was or even who he was. He just was, and for the first time in the history of any thinking creature, this was enough.

The voice of Lady Narwhal sounded in his head. "That's enough hanging around, doll. You've got work to do."

At once, the darkness took on different hues, lightening in some places and thickening in others, swirling about and reforming and solidifying into different shapes. After an age or a moment—Dalmaan could not tell which—a definitive environment surrounded him.

High above, swirls of magnificent colors streaked hauntingly across a dark-purple sky; emerald green flecked with yellow and pink and other hues Dalmaan could put no name to seemed lit from within, more insubstantial than clouds. Where he stood, it was crystal of a dazzling white, sparkling like the brightest of starry skies. Beyond, he could see places where it was greener than the lights in the sky, and in still other places it undulated into massive spires, towering cliffs of ice.

"What is this place?" As he asked he looked round for the Lady Narwhal, but she was nowhere to be seen. "Lady? Where am I?"

Once more her voice, without a source, sounded in his mind. "Right where you were, and somewhere else entirely."

"What does that mean?"

"It means that I don't have the words to properly tell you what this place is."

"Is it real?"

"Realer than your world, sweetie, but nowhere near as interesting, I admit. Now you know what you have to do."

"I do?"

"Of course. Find your brother, and take him out of himself."

"But he is in the village, in the healer's tent!"

"Yes, and he's also here."

"Where?" Dalmaan looked dubiously at his surroundings. "This place is endless! Where could I even start?"

"Start where you are, and keep going till the end. That's the long and the short of it."

"Lady, this is nonsense!"

"The only kind of sense worth your time is your own, doll." The Lady's voice grew fainter as she continued. "You've spent your whole life betting on certainties, Dalmaan. For once, give uncertainty a try. Trust me—it's more rewarding and a hell of a lot more fun."

As the voice faded completely, Dalmaan's fear began to rise.

"Don't leave me to this! Ladyship? Ladyship!"

Nothing. Dalmaan was alone in the mysterious realm.

He stood there for a time, looking around, trying to decide on where he should go. Finally, apprehensively, he set off for the west, where the ground sloped down easily into a deep ravine.

He carefully edged his way down the smooth decline, keeping his balance and cursing his lack of a weapon. The walls of the crevasse seemed to glow from within by the same cerulean light he had seen in Lady Narwhal's cavern, and Dalmaan felt his apprehension subside slightly.

He began to hear a slight thrumming. A stream, perhaps? But no, it seemed too organized a sound to be natural. He could detect a regular rhythm to it, and caught himself humming along. It was a song, and it was a woman singing.

As he continued, the voice seemed to echo about the crevasse, coming from everywhere at once. He could not discern the words, but he could understand the emotions behind it. There was melancholy, certainly, but also a burning joy. There was sadness sung not as an impediment to joy but as an expression of joy. He could feel the loss of love as a revelation of value, the escape into the self, and the comfort of the final end, when anything that might matter would be over and done with, feeling as he listened as though a burden he had carried all his life had finally lifted from his shoulders. He could hear this, and he could understand this.

He shivered at the voice, feminine and haunting yet melodious and passionate. Several times he thought he had glimpsed the singer from the corner of his eye as a lithe shape with a rampant mop of raven hair, but it disappeared when he turned.

"Hello?" It seemed blasphemous to call out in this place of such soulful music, but it did not stop at the sound of his voice. "I need...I'm looking for my brother. Lady Narwhal sent me."

Still the music did not stop. Instead, it traveled forward, deeper into the canyon. Dalmaan, heartened at this, raced to follow the siren song. He ran in pursuit of the phantom songstress.

At last, the crevasse ended, rather abruptly, in a massive wall of ice so dark it was nearly black. At its base was a chipped and ragged hole—a deep cave. A section of ice protruded over the entrance, and standing on this with nimble toes was the Songstress.

She was a shadowy form, nearly invisible before the endless black of the wall. Her clothes were billowing shades, and blurred much of her features. He could just make out an elfin face, sorrowful yet kind, beneath a wild head of ebony hair.

The Songstress continued to sing, and knelt at the lip of the cavern. She waved an arm languidly to Dalmaan, indicating for him to continue onward. As he passed beneath her she brushed her hand across his cheek, and in that instant he knew everything she felt. He knew the world as cruel, and the strength it took not to despair. He knew the utter emptiness of the cosmos, and the blindness of human desire. But beyond that, he felt something pure, and good. It was hope, but not a naïve hope. It was mature, and wise to the capriciousness of fate, and all the greater for it. This was something his brother knew without realizing, always making light of life even when things were at their worst. Not ignoring woe, or denying it; simply carrying it along and dancing beneath the weight.

Dalmaan stumbled into the cave and fell to his knees, overcome with this enlightenment. His cry of despair choked halfway into a manic laugh, and tears of both sadness and happiness stung his eyes. Was it really that simple? This was the knowledge that made Vagn content with the way things were? It was so obvious, a child could understand it!

He stood up and, in this fit of realization, ran on, whooping into the darkness, caution forgotten. Besides, he could see lights far ahead. Several of them seemed to move about as he approached, and as he arrived he realized this was because they were, in fact, moving.

They were tiny squids, floating and glowing with the now-familiar blue light he had seen in the crevasse. Their tentacles were spider-thin, and propelled them as they swam in the blackness. He could see their eyes—minute orbs staring at him with alien bemusement. One drifted in front of his face, and he held out his palm.

It spun there, tentacles undulating as it regarded him, and swam away. Several more began to float about his shoulders and along his arms, seemingly playful and curious about this new visitor. Dalmaan's awe, already long since palpable, was threatening to cloud his reason completely. He could have been perfectly content to abandon the journey for Vagn and stay in the cave with these strange new friends.

But…no. He gathered his wits and whispered, so as not to frighten the squids away, "I am looking for my brother. Is he here? The Lady of Narwhals sent me."

At the mention of Lady Narwhal, the squids stopped and floated motionless. Then, as one, they drifted further down the cave. Dalmaan followed.

The squids' glow could only illuminate a little of the path ahead. There were voices in the dark; there were sighs and whispers, just beyond hearing—murmurs of comfort and sing-song rasps that chanted nonsense.

Dalmaan felt no fear of them.

Finally, the darkness began to thin, and Dalmaan could see human forms in various positions all around him. Most lay prostrate on unseen surfaces. Some stood, arms crossed over their chests. Others knelt, like supplicants before unseen forces, arms over their heads, backs exposed to elements he could only guess at.

"Vagn!"

He was curled into a ball, hugging his knees. His eyes were shut tight, tears leaking from the sides and streaming down his cheeks. He was whimpering, and shivering. Dalmaan's ebullience fled him at the sight; he had found Vagn in this position before, woken in the night by bad dreams. He had always let their mother deal with him in such circumstances.

He knelt before his little brother, and very gently laid a hand on his shoulder. Vagn gave no reaction, and Dalmaan began to feel sick with fear.

"Vagn. I'm here. It's okay. We're leaving now. Let's get you home, brother."

Vagn shook his head, still whispering to himself inaudibly. Dalmaan strained to listen.

"What is it? Open your eyes."

"It's dark." Vagn's voice was tiny and broken, and utterly afraid. "So dark. I can't see."

Dalmaan tried to be reasonable, and spoke softly. "Vagn, it's dark because your eyes are closed. There is light here, I promise. Just open your eyes, and you will see it."

Vagn shook his head, and did not open his eyes.

Before, Dalmaan would have become short with his little brother's stubbornness. Now he knew how to change his mind. He reached up to a squid floating above his head. The little creature sat on his hand, and he held it in front of his brother's face.

Vagn opened his eyes at this sudden intrusion of light and gasped in astonishment. "So beautiful!"

Dalmaan felt immensely relieved. This was his brother, enamored with the beauty of things, looking beyond the unfamiliar nature of the most unusual sights and able to process the absurd without fearing it.

Vagn stared at the floating squid as Dalmaan tapped him on the shoulder.

"There are many others, brother. Come see."

For only a second, Vagn hesitated, and then, glancing once more at the squid, he grinned his familiar wide and excited grin and took his brother's hand.

What a show those squids performed for the brothers as they left the cave! Both of them were equally wide in eyes and mouths as the creatures zoomed and swooshed in the heights of the cavern, their light streaming behind them. They whirled into fantastic patterns, formed illuminated shapes—a night sky, each squid spreading its tentacles to imitate the stars; a whirling ribbon of cephalopods; a fantastically massive wheel, spinning slowly amongst the stalactites.

For their final act, the squids spun together at immense speed, seeming to meld into each other until floating above was a massive and swirled narwhal's horn—a celestial Stabby Thing—pointing the way to the exit.

As they stepped outside the cave, Dalmaan saw immediately they were somewhere else. A wide shore stretched in both directions, and the night's darkness was greater than before. The only source of the blue glow was a medium-sized ice floe sitting in the ocean directly opposite them, just large enough for the two of them to stand on.

The Songstress stood poised at the other end of the floe, her back to the brothers and her arms spread wide, as though she imagined herself the figurehead on the prow of a mighty ship. Dalmaan touched Vagn's shoulder and cautioned him to keep his distance—some things were too perfect to approach.

The very second they stepped onto the ice floe the Songstress began to sing once more and stepped forward. As she ran, similar ice floes appeared beneath her feet, creating a pathway over the water. Vagn whooped and ran after her, not seeming to notice the ice form beneath his feet, so enamored was he by her music.

Dalmaan pursued him, shouting, "I'll get you yet, you little terror!" Yet he was not frightened or annoyed by his brother's behavior, as had once been the case. Now he laughed along with him, thrilled beyond measure to see Vagn's ecstatic grin, and to hear his happy squealing as he fled. From that day, he knew he would live for that smile, and that laugh.

They ran—the warrior made a child again after the child who had remade him. Together, they pursued the unattainable beauty in the wake of her sorrowful song.

Dalmaan caught up to Vagn and swung the giggling youth onto his shoulders, not breaking his stride. He held onto his brother's legs, loping across the sea as Vagn hurrahed with his hands in the air.

They came to the last of the floes, the Songstress now nowhere in sight. Dalmaan felt Vagn's laughter wheeze into awed silence, and he smiled at the Lady of Narwhals, swimming casually in the water and gazing up at them.

"The narwhal..." Vagn whispered. Now that the magnificent creature he had glimpsed by chance sat before him, he seemed too overcome to speak.

"The narwhal is right!" Lady Narwhal laughed, pleased at Vagn's stupefied look. "Nice to see your big bro pulling his weight for once. I swear, you two are too adorable for words!"

"Don't be alarmed, brother. She often talks like this," Dalmaan grinned mischievously up at Vagn. "He seems rather overcome, Ladyship!"

"I have that effect on boys." The Lady winked, and Vagn giggled behind his hands. "As much fun as this has been, I'm afraid it's time I sent you boys home. Your mama wouldn't thank me for keeping you both out all night."

"Must we leave already?" Vagn spread his hands wide to encompass the all-surrounding sea. "There's so much to explore here!"

"Afraid so, hon. Too much of a good thing wears hard on the soul, and this place is too good by half. It takes a special kind of person to live here indefinitely."

Dalmaan thought of the willowy form and sad smile of the Songstress and felt moved to agree. Lady Narwhal caught his eye knowingly.

"She was smothered in the real world. It took skies like these for her to bloom properly."

"Will we ever see you again, My Lady?"

For a moment, the radiant Narwhal seemed somber, and the aura of sheer life that blanketed her dimmed a little. She recovered herself and replied offhandedly, "Well, I might stop by every now and again. If I'm wanted. And if there's some good wine going spare." Then, very quietly: "Live for the day, toots. Live for the day."

The sea began to bubble and froth, and the ice floe started to sink. Dalmaan was not surprised that he did not feel the chill of the cold sea against his legs. He was accustomed to miracles by now.

"You'd better stick with the big lug, sweetie," the Lady told Vagn. "Your brother needs someone with better eyes to see. And you, just occasionally, need someone with a better head." She laughed, and the brothers laughed with her. They both reached out to touch her as they sank beneath the waves.

—◆—

"Dalmaan! Whatever are you doing in here?"

Dalmaan rose to groggy alertness, his head seeming too heavy for his neck. His joints were cramped and achy; he had been sleeping in a fetal position on the ground.

Liza glared at him sternly. "What do you think you were doing, sleeping in here? Your brother needs to heal."

"I—I was just..." What *was* he doing? He was at the shore, of that he was certain. There had been water. Had he been swimming? He had pinched the bridge of his nose and was attempting to summon some explanation for his mother when they both heard a noise.

"Mama..." Vagn's voice was hoarse and small. He coughed a wet, brackish cough and clutched the air. "Mama, are you there?"

Liza rushed to his bedside and knelt beside him. He opened his eyes and smiled up at her. Her eyes streamed with tears as she clutched him tightly.

"You little fool!" she cried. "What were you thinking of, scaring me like that?"

Vagn saw his brother over their mother's shoulder and smiled. And Dalmaan *remembered*.

He remembered a journey beneath a sky alive with cold fire. He remembered an elusive Songstress, alone in her music yet content to be alive. He remembered stars that swam and water that did not chill. And he remembered dark, kind eyes behind the magnificent curl of a Stabby Thing.

When Vagn had been fed and regained some of his strength he wasted no time in telling Liza of the other world, and the Lady Narwhal.

"It was real, Mama!" Vagn protested, although his mother did not chide him, and only answered with her sparkling laugh. "There was a bright, colorful sky, and flying squid, and a strange singing woman, and the narwhal helped us, and it was real!"

"I'm sure it was." Liza was smiling despite her red-rimmed eyes, happy to have both of her sons in her arms.

"Dalmaan was there as well! He can tell you!"

"It's true," Dalmaan whispered, surprising both Liza and Vagn. "I was, there was, and she did."

"Well!" Liza was bemused at this unlikely behavior, not sure what to make of the change. Still, things that were meant were no business of hers, and how could she argue with the evidence of this miraculous camaraderie between her boys? "Then all I can say is that I am deeply grateful to this Lady of Narwhals for showing my sons the way home from such strange lands."

And the brothers smiled at each other, and said no more.

In the years that followed the brothers Dalmaan and Vagn were nearly inseparable, and so alike as to be nigh indistinguishable. Vagn would still play his games; Dalmaan, when he was not engaged in village matters, would join him. He would chase and leap after him across the boulders, catching him and spinning him about by his legs, joining in the games of hide-and-seek and mock battles he staged with the other children. This also had the unintended effect of strengthening Dalmaan's position in the village—the other adults could not help but be warmed by this man who, although once considered rather stuffy and pompous, would now step aside from his serious responsibilities to run about with their children.

Vagn, meanwhile, gained his own special position among the village council. Who could have guessed that young man would become one of their tribe's most important diplomats as he grew? In times of conflict between neighboring villages Vagn's word was highly valued. When tempers had all but broken down communications Vagn would arrive, his cool but shrewd reasoning adding a great amount of levity to any discussion, bringing the most opposed of leaders together in unprecedented brotherhood. By his hand the tribes grew together and prospered until they were well on the way to becoming the massive family we know today.

But what united the peoples, more than anything, what made them set aside their differences of petty pride and honor to live for the day, were the stories of the Lady of Narwhals. For hours, Vagn would keep his audience enthralled, sitting together round the fire, entranced at his tales of the Wielder of the Stabby, the playful goddess beneath the sea who demanded no sacrifice other than one's doubt and fear, who wanted nothing of her people but for them to be happy and having a good time (and perhaps the occasional drink).

From those days onward every village within the nation of Stingandi would erect its own Stabby Thing. Houses bore them as spires on their roofs, and the village centers were marked by beautifully curved monuments of stone or wood, impaling the sky and declaring to one and all that here was a place to have a good time.

From this *Náhvalur Nótt* was born. Song echoes across the continent, brilliant pyres of green and blue shock the night, and the streets are alive with children and adults, dancing and shrieking and laughing at the sheer wonderment of being alive, and together.

And on every shore, cooling in the water, one will likely find a simple earthenware jug of the very finest wine—an invitation to the Lady herself. And maybe one may glimpse, if one has sharp eyes and a strong head, the shimmering of blue light on the water, the sound of a splash, and the glint of moonlight on an ivory horn.

In a cavern that stretches beneath the streets —all streets, everywhere—amongst stacks of words abandoned as soon as they were composed, the wretched story thief was wailing.

The thing in his arms could no longer be called a manuscript; it was a collective, cancerous mess of papers, flung together and falling apart. Many were escaping behind D'shall in an untidy trail, and he despaired of recovering them. Surely, he had enough now anyway? Surely, somewhere in here was his fortune. If only he could find the way out!

You are told from an early age that you can make of the world whatever you want of it, but the truth is the world will make whatever it wants of you. The world is a vicious, ravening machine that grinds even the sturdiest cogs into dust, always chaotic and unswayable. It does not care for your sorrows; it will not try and ease your pains. Nobody else will, either. They've got their own to deal with.

The writers were laughing at him, he knew it. Those self-righteous whiners, those incorrigible children who refused to mature! They were all of them in on it, from that pathetic worm Bell all the way up to that harpy, that gorger on the carrion of will, the old woman. Even now they were surely hiding in the stacks as they had been all along, stifling their giggles amid the shifting, musty paper.

That is what set you on this path—the realization that to create a dam against a torrent is not enough.

But look what he had done! Look what D'shall, who hadn't taken up the pen in decades, had achieved! He'd breached their stronghold, their throwaway bin of high expectations, and was going to make a masterpiece! More fool they, who wasted ink as others wasted breath, tossing it away as if it mattered, as if the world weren't full of impressionable, gullible mites who wouldn't know a good story if it was written in the dirt beneath their feet. Well, they were his now, and those suffering divas would surely thank him for making them wiser.

You have a pain that has grown into determination, and if you ever think to lift your head above your own grieving heart you may find others who feel the same.

The stacks of paper were coming apart, but that was all right. They were spilling out of his hands. All around was only walls, but not to worry! Sooner or later, the door would reveal itself.

D'shall leaned against yet another wall of stone, breathing deeply, clutching the ever more crumpled stories to his chest. The light was fading, surely?

Ahead, from deep within the Library, there came a noise.

The scratch of paper. The rusty chuckle of a dried, parchment throat.

The rising roar as a million stacks of paper fell apart, sending their fellows toppling like dominos.

A tide of dust and skin and wounds that wept.

Stillness.

Above all, let your pain bleed through.

END

ABOUT THE AUTHOR

DANIEL HALE is an storyteller living in Ohio. An ardent bibliophile and aspiring Anglophile, when not writing he spends his time acquiring books faster than he can read them and perfecting his British accent. He has been published in several anthologies, including *All Hallow's Evil* and *Strangely Funny III* by Mystery and Horror, LLC, *What Has Two Heads, Ten Eyes, and Terrifying Table Manners?*, by Mega Thump Publishing, *The Last Diner* by Knight Watch Press, *Creature Stew* by Papa Bear Publications, and *The Myriad Carnival* by Glitter Wolf Publications. He is also a three-time competitor in the Writer's Area.

ABOUT THE ARTISTS

BOB HOBBS has been a professional illustrator for more than 30 years. His work has graced the published short stories of such celebrated authors as Ursula K. LeGuin, Larry Niven, Algis Budrys, Yves Maynard, Alexander Jablokov, Lawrence Watt Evans and more. and has appeared in dozens of magazines such as *Amazing Stories*, *Tomorrow SF*, *Figment*, *On Spec* and *Talebones*. His illustrations have appeared in *Drawing and Painting Fantasy Worlds* by Finlay Cowan, *The Fantasy Art Bible* by Jane Moseley, *Phantastic Faeries* and *Dark Art* by Bob Hobbs, and *The Star Trek Concordance* by Bjo Trimble, to name a few. He has also done game-related work for such companies as Wizards of the Coast, Flying Buffalo and Steve Jackson Games.

  Bob has been listed in the *Marquis Who's Who in America* four times, is an L. Ron Hubbard Illustrators of the Future winner and received an American InHouse Design Award as part of the creative team behind the Zombie Pandemic graphic novella.

APRIL MARTINEZ was born in the Philippines and raised in San Diego, California, daughter to a US Navy chef and a US postal worker. Dissatisfied that she couldn't make use of her creative tendencies, she started working as an imaging specialist for a big book and magazine publishing house in Irvine learned the trade of graphic design. From that point on, she worked as a graphic designer and webmaster while doing freelance art and illustration at night. April lives with her cat in Orange County, California.`

www.ingramcontent.com/pod-product-compliance
Lightning Source LLC
Chambersburg PA
CBHW031958240626
47153CB00003B/1029